CW00450003

GREAT IS HIS

C. BORDEN

C.B. WRITING SOLUTIONS

Cover Design: C.B. Writing Solutions

Editor: Lisa Binion

Genre: Christian Fiction; Historical Fiction

❀ Created with Vellum

Above all, I need to thank my Lord God and Savior for helping me write this. The Lord placed men and women in my path along this journey who acted as prayer partners, beta readers, accountability partners, and ARC Reviewers: all who helped me make this book an acceptable offering for Him to use to draw people to His message of faithful love to us.

Therefore, I dedicate this book to the men and women who linked arms with me in big ways and small despite living busy lives of their own:

Astrid, Cyndi, Elizabeth, Ethan, Jackie, Kearsie, Lisa, Marsha, Meloni, Michael, Sonya, Tabitha, and those few who have asked to remain nameless.

I am forever grateful for each of you!

FROM THE AUTHOR

Greetings,

Writing this book has taken me on an unexpected journey.

This is, of course, a fictional accounting of what I imagine happened in the spaces of Ruth that were not mentioned within the Biblical account. I often wondered about the relationship between Naomi and Ruth.

Why would Naomi call herself bitter?

What was the extent of her sorrow?

Beyond her sorrow and bitterness, why did Ruth choose to remain with Naomi rather than return to her own people?

And why on earth would lying at Boaz's feet cause the man to become enamored with Ruth and seek her hand in marriage?

I know I am not the first to wonder these things, and I know a great many writers have researched and sought to fill in the gaps to gain better understanding. Within the many months of research and cross-referencing and re-researching aspects of Ruth's account and where her story fits into Biblical history, I would have been remiss to ignore the cultural aspects of the time she lived. Throughout this fictional representation, I add bits of Hebrew terminology, touches of cultural aspects, and unexpected historical notes that inspired much of how I imagined Ruth's story to play out.

Even as I tried to keep the story as culturally and historically accurate as well as true to the Biblical message and purpose, I uncovered a great many controversies and dilemmas presented within the Book of Ruth that were affected by translation, interpretation, and imposition of texts outside accepted Scripture. For that reason, I have included a glossary of terms and a bibliography at the end of this book. For all those things within this accounting that may seem odd or an excessive stretch of the imagination, I encourage you to consult the many books and websites I used for my research. Prayerfully consider how those sources compare to Scripture.

Plus, I beg you to forgive me: I did not cite each source within the narrative itself for fear of pulling you out of the story. However, I tried to *italicize* the first examples of terms that are featured in the glossary. For example: the first time I use *Ephrathah* in chapter one, I italicized it and referred to it in the glossary as the original name for the city of Bethlehem. Similarly, other Hebrew terms will be italicized the first time I use them.

I sincerely pray this novel drives you to read the <u>Book of Ruth</u> and the Holy Bible so you can know our God as a personal companion and a perfect redeemer.

God bless you,

C. Borden

CONTENTS

PART ONE: NAOMI

*In the days when the judges ruled, there was a famine
in the land. So a man from Ephrathah in
Judah, together with his wife and two sons, went
to live for a while in the country of Moab. The
man's name was Elimelek, his wife's name was
Naomi, and the names of his two sons were
Mahlon and Kilion. They were Ephrathites from
Ephrathah, Judah. And they went to Moab and
lived there.*

*Now Elimelek, Naomi's husband, died, and she was
left with her two sons. They married Moabite
women, one named Orpah and the other
Ruth. After they had lived there about ten
years, both Mahlon and Kilion also died, and
Naomi was left without her two sons and her
husband.*

When Naomi heard in Moab that the Lord had come

to the aid of his people by providing food for them, she and her daughters-in-law prepared to return home from there...

But Naomi said, "Return home, my daughters..."
But Ruth replied, "Don't urge me to leave you..."
Ruth 1: 1-6, 11, 16

ONE

Our caravan stopped at the top of the rise that overlooked our small town of *Ephrathah*. I sat alone at the head of a small cart, determined not to look back at the only home I'd ever known. We'd never ventured far from Ephrathah. To leave now with my aging husband and our grown sons, I was more frightened than I'd ever been of the famine itself. I prayed we were making the right decision though I knew my husband was convinced we had to leave.

After years of struggling through the long famine, Elimelek had had enough. He was so determined to reverse our fortunes; he didn't even make the time to consult with the city elders as he should have.

I gripped my hands tightly in my lap and closed my eyes as I whispered yet another prayer to *Yahweh*.

I'd voiced my many concerns to Elimelek in the night when we were alone, when the rest of the house had long gone to bed. I'd told him how deeply I feared moving would prove to be a greater burden on our family than it would be to remain and trust God to provide as He had done without fail.

Still there I sat, alone on the cart while Elimelek and our sons, Mahlon and Kilion, as well as a few of our remaining servants, drove what was left of our herds slowly behind me. I clicked my tongue at the oxen pulling the overfull cart and sighed with them as they lumbered back to a start.

Still determined not to look back, instead, I listened hard for the sounds of my town rising behind us. I heard the chatter of people, the distant laughter of women and children despite the hardships they were facing. Someone down there was singing a haunting melody, the notes of the song barely carried on the winds up to where I sat. The ghostly notes caused the skin on my arms to prickle. Again, I closed my eyes and let the sounds wash over me, drinking them in, storing them away in my heart. Meanwhile, the oxen plodded along, rattling and jolting the cart under me.

Lord, will we ever see our home again?

"Naomi, can you spur the oxen to move a little faster? The herds are eager to be on their way."

I glanced to the side to see Elimelek walking beside the cart. It struck me how much he still affected me; he was still very handsome even though gray filled his beard and touched his temples and was still very strong despite the sacrifices he made daily to keep us fed and cared for. He walked with his back straight and his gaze proud, his trusty staff in hand. Beyond the physical pull I felt to him, I knew it was more than looks alone. He exuded confidence and security, and he expected my support.

I nodded in silence and snapped the whip against the oxen's rears.

I was still perturbed with him. He chose not to heed my advice or take my ideas to heart. The way he had grown used to making decisions without me hurt more deeply than it should have, but our early marriage had been shaped on shared decisions. We worked together, not apart.

But Elimelek was a proud man. He didn't see the small miracles Yahweh provided us with every day. He saw his flocks growing leaner and the herds dwindling. When our servants lost their children to starvation, he mourned with them. He watched our sons become weak and ill with no interest in living life and no interest in furthering their lineage.

Plus, I knew how deeply it bothered him that he was expected to offer aid and help when asked entirely because of his standing within the community. He was not an elder, but he was a landowner, and as such, he had responsibilities beyond our family.

I sighed to myself as I recalled the beginning of the famine. At first, Elimelek offered aid freely without regret, but as our family suffered more and more, his ability to help others meant more we had to sacrifice food ourselves. After a while, he'd grown weary of giving aid to those even less fortunate than us. As his reluctance became more apparent, our elders called him to account for his increasing stinginess.

In his eyes, what our family needed was a fresh start. He thought Moab offered an opportunity to replenish our wealth, revitalize our family, and put an end to the suffering. Removing ourselves from the scrutiny of the elders and the never-ending needs of those in want of food added to his desire to leave. Thus, my many objections fell on deaf ears. I didn't understand him. Nor did I understand the war raging in me as I fought to be obedient to my God and also to my husband.

Angrily, I flicked the short crop in my hands at the backsides of the oxen, and they moved at a faster pace. I knew Elimelek could sense my simmering frustration with him.

"Come, *Isha*. Look down there. Don't you see? It's all withered and dry. There's nothing for us anymore. There hasn't been for a long time now."

I refused to look at where he was pointing. He was right as far as the famine went. There were no crops being grown anywhere. This meant there was not enough grain for our bread, and there wasn't enough grain to feed the livestock. Once abundant fields had long grown brown with dry and brittle stalks. Many were mostly sandy plots where not even weeds found enough moisture to grow.

Despite the truth of the hardship we'd been living under, I still felt we were wrong to leave. This place was more than simply a thirsty land. Ephrathah, the land of Judah, was our home and our history. It was our heritage and our culture. This was where our God had brought our people, but my husband knew my feelings on the matter. He was not swayed.

Elimelek continued to walk beside the cart. After a while, he reached up and took one of my hands in his own. "We are bound, Isha. I know you don't like this move, but you'll see. We'll make a new life. I will see to it."

The unspoken plea in his voice was obvious. He needed my support. He needed me to believe in him. Even if I thought we were wrong to leave, the fact was, I did believe in him. I trusted him to keep us safe and do the best he could to care for us.

Glancing at him, I stared deeply into his dark brown eyes flecked with specks of green and gold. There was no anger in his eyes though I knew he had every right to be angry with my coldness. The love reflected in his eyes melted my anger away, just as it always did. I squeezed his hand gently. He hated for me to be upset with him, and when he looked at me like that, I found it hard to remain angry with him.

I sighed. I loved him so deeply. "So long as we are together," I commented lightly.

Elimelek grinned. The young man I grew to love long ago was reflected in that grin. "So long as we are together," he echoed.

He pulled my hand toward him and kissed it before he let it go. Looking back at me and then ahead to the road in front of us, he beamed.

"Do you think you can get these stubborn creatures to move any faster? I'd like to be a fair distance before we bed for the night."

I couldn't resist the challenge anymore than I could resist the power of his smile. Nodding, I replied, "Of course I can get them to move faster."

I felt a smirk touch my lips, and I flicked the rears of the oxen again, calling out a command to them. They moved at a near trot, leaving Elimelek standing in dust surrounded by the goats he was driving forward.

"That's the spirit!" he called after me.

As the road stretched before me, I felt the weight of my fears settle on my heart once more. It didn't take long for me to get lost deep in my more negative thoughts. The day moved from morning to afternoon to night, and Ephrathah grew farther and farther behind us.

TWO

I woke with the sun shining warmly on my face through the open flap of the tent. The heavy pounding of hammers was coming from somewhere nearby. With a deep breath, I stretched and got up from the thickly padded bedroll and looked out the open flap of the tent we slept in. My faithful handmaid, Terah, sat next to the fire working on something in one of the clay pots. There didn't appear to be anyone else about. I smoothed my hair and began braiding it as I stepped out of the tent into the already scorching morning sun.

"Why did no one wake me?" I asked Terah.

The aging woman stopped her work and bowed her head slightly toward me. "Master Elimelek told me to let you sleep this morning."

When I finished braiding my hair, I threw it over my shoulder. I covered my head with a thin shawl, thankful for the shade it offered my eyes. I looked around the campsite and saw dirty dishes yet to be gathered up.

"Did you set aside some food for me?"

Terah nodded and moved to fetch it while I set about gathering the dirty plates and clay cups scattered around. When Terah returned with a plate of flat bread, a boiled egg, and some dried meat, I set the dishes down and took the plate as I thanked Terah. Terah merely nodded, never a woman to waste words. Then she gathered the dishes into her arms and walked away to take care of them. With my mouth full, I motioned for her to pause and I sat down.

After swallowing, I asked her, "Where are the men?"

She glanced up the hill to the south. "They are working on the house."

Frustration bubbled inside me. I followed her gaze up the hill. From where I sat, I couldn't see anything, but I could hear the noise of men working. We'd only been in Moab a little over a month after taking nearly a month to travel from Ephrathah. Elimelek had seen a little green and a bit of water running in a tiny stream, and he claimed the land for his own. We'd already had disputes with the local Moabites who were used to allowing their goats and sheep to roam freely over the landscape. After much persuasion and a bit of bribing, Elimelek convinced our new neighbors to recognize his claim on the land.

Again, without talking to me. Again, without praying about this with our family, I thought.

I shook my head and looked toward the sun. The heat was intense, but I liked to think Yahweh was in the light, in the warmth, bringing comfort and life into me. I stood in the sun for several minutes, forcing myself to shake off the frustration and bitterness. Then I bowed my head to pray over my family and our new home. And I prayed, yet again, for the Lord to call us back to Ephrathah.

After I finished praying, I got up and took my plate to Terah.

"See these are done quickly. Then air out the tents today. I'd also like to have all the bedding and linens hung out to be refreshed."

"I will see to it," Terah responded.

Without another word, confident she would gather the other women to see the work done, I picked up a walking stick and strolled up the hill to see what progress the men were making. Once I crested the top, I watched them for several minutes.

I was astonished by how much had been done already. The walls were nearly as tall as me; mud and clay formed bricks similar to what we had used to build within Ephrathah. I observed the careful way the men carried and set the bricks one on another. Moving around to the front of the structure, I noticed several of the local women and children were seated on the ground watching and pointing. There were few permanent settlements among the Moabites, and in that specific area where Elimelek laid his claim, the people were mostly nomadic. Some, mainly the women and children, had never set foot in the small towns that were spread across the land, so the building of a permanent structure fascinated them.

"Ah, Naomi! You're awake."

A smile spread across my face without even thinking, and I turned to greet Elimelek. "My love, it's coming along quickly."

Elimelek embraced me, kissing me on my forehead, and I melted into his arms. He held me for a moment, then he stepped away and called out, "Mahlon! You and your brother come here."

My smile grew as I watched my sons separate from the men at work. Both of their thin bodies were covered in wet and drying mud and clay. They were notably stronger than they had been just two months earlier. The famine had robbed them of much of their strength, and while we were in Ephrathah, I had feared they would never recover.

Thank you, Lord. Is this a sign that we are indeed where you want us to be?

"*Ima!*" Mahlon tried to wipe the mud off his hands. After several failed attempts, he simply leaned in and pecked me on the cheek. "*Boker tov!*"

Kilion looked at his muddy hands and arms then at me. I saw the flash of mischief in his eyes. Before I could tell him no, he grabbed me in a crushing hug that picked me up off the ground. "Boker tov, Ima!"

Elimelek laughed as I demanded to be put down. After Kilion set me back on my feet, I tried to wipe the mud off my robe.

"Oh, you..." I started but stopped when Kilion pecked me on the cheek with a quick laugh. Throwing my hands up, I complained, "I can't win."

"Boys, tell your Ima the exciting news."

I looked from Elimelek to our sons. My heart skipped a beat immediately hoping word had come that my prayers were answered, and we were going home. But as soon as I thought it, I knew that was not it, or my men would not still be building a house. Even as disappointment blossomed, I forced myself to remain enthusiastic about whatever the news was. I continued to smile though I was certain they could tell it was no longer sincere.

Mahlon used the corner of his *halug* to wipe the sweat from his face and then spoke up, "We've got word that King Eglon will pass through this area."

I cringed inwardly. "The significance of his passing through is...?"

Elimelek replied, "The significance is that he's heard of us. He's coming specifically to speak to me."

I couldn't help the frown that instantly took the place of my smile. "This is good news?"

My mind raced as I considered the angry words and near fights we'd already experienced with the local people. Had the local people made a complaint that reached the king's ears? The king of Moab was not known to be a man of peace. From the way the men in Ephrathah spoke of him, he was a man jealous of the Israelites, a man eager to weave his way into our God-given land.

Elimelek continued, "I've been assured that he means us no harm. He's not bringing an army. He is coming with just a small retinue. I gather he's curious about us."

I worked hard to keep my voice calm. "I see. So you think meeting him is a good thing? He's not of our people. What if he means to impose his gods on us? What if he intends to use us to gain information about our land? Or what if his intentions are to enslave us? Have you thought of that?"

Silence.

My boys shuffled their feet awkwardly. They avoided looking at me or Elimelek. That's when I saw that Elimelek's face was red, the muscle in his jaw twitching as he clenched his teeth. I bowed my head in sudden embarrassment. I hadn't intended to question him in front of people. But I'd allowed my worries to affect me, and I forgot myself. Worse, I'd questioned Elimelek in front of our sons, our servants, and the Moabite strangers. I felt the color drain from my face as the redness in his face grew darker.

Sternly and loudly, he replied, "The king will be here in a week. I expect you to see that we are prepared for his presence." Without another word, Elimelek turned on his heel and stomped away, leaving our sons to stare after him sheepishly.

I stepped up to our boys and put a hand on each of them. "I guess he wants the structure to be completed in time for this king's visit?"

Mahlon nodded, careful to avoid my searching stare.

"Very well. I know he'll see it done. You both go help him. I'll see that we are prepared to move in as soon as it is ready."

I leaned up and kissed them both on their muddy faces. Then I watched them as they moved back to the mud, clay, and water while my husband took his anger out on a wooden beam.

I continued watching them for a few moments as my anger grew. Had I just been ambushed by my husband? Surely, he had known how learning of a visit from the Moabite ruler would affect me. After all, he knew my concerns regarding living among the gentiles. Did he tell me now in front of all these people, knowing I was not supposed to react except with outward subservience? If he thought this meant I would not be addressing this again tonight when we were alone, he had to know he was wrong.

Tears of frustration welled up in my eyes, and my throat got tight. I took several deep breaths and wiped my eyes before I allowed myself the pleasure of stomping down the hill to take out my frustration on some blankets that were surely already airing out.

THREE

The caravan stopped a short distance from where we had set up camp when Elimelek chose to build there. Behind me, servants were erecting several tents for people to gather under to escape the heat of the sun, but I paid them no attention. My attention was entirely on the royal retinue below. The caravan was larger than I'd expected.

As they entered the valley, I had counted the number of men on camels, followed by covered carts I assumed carried women and children. Behind them were armed men on horseback and more armed men on foot. Then at the end of the procession, numerous servants drove heavy-laden carts with supplies or helped herd small droves of goats, sheep, and fowl. I watched as they stopped and began setting up tents of their own. A small group of men stood apart from the flurry of activity, and I assumed among them was King Eglon, king of Moab.

"He's here."

I jumped in surprise as Elimelek stepped to my side. "Will we be ready to receive him this evening?"

I nodded. "Yes. If the Moabite will even consider our request."

Elimelek gave me a sideways glance. I wasn't sure I cared if he heard the disapproving tone in my voice.

"Naomi, he is the ruler of this land. If we hope to remain here for even a little while, we need his blessing. His people will follow his lead. If he doesn't give us his blessing, we will have to return to our tents and move on," he paused and took a breath, "even farther from Ephrathah."

I snapped my head to look at him, anger causing me to bite my lip to hold back my response. The look on my husband's face held no room for argument and impressed upon me his expectations should the king visit with us. I sucked in my breath deeply. I had much to say, but I knew my words would have to wait. Forcing myself to remain calm, I took a deep breath and looked back down at the caravan. "We better send someone down with the invitation then."

Elimelek nodded in agreement. "Yes. I'll go myself." He paused, shook his head, and amended, "No. I will go with Mahlon. We will be nonthreatening, just the two of us plus a couple servants, I think."

I frowned as I eyed the armed men below them. "Are you sure it's safe?"

Elimelek shrugged. "Probably not, but our people have had fair negotiations with the Moabites in the past. For all his conniving, the king is not known to be a rash man. I'm sure we will be fine."

I faced him. "What are you taking to present as a gift?"

Elimelek smiled widely. "A small box of our finest herbs from Ephrathah. A couple jars of oil. One of the newborn sheep. Humble gifts but fine gifts."

"Very well. You better hurry so I know how much food we need to make for his visit."

Elimelek stared at me for a few seconds, trying to read my mood. He knew I was saving my fight with him for later, but I'm sure he sensed more in my mood than mere disapproval.

Was I disappointed in him? Oh yes. I was more disappointed in him now that we were finally in a place where there was food and moisture and the possibility to once again prosper than I had ever been in Ephrathah when I worried over every crumb. I knew my worries and doubts made no sense to him. He did not understand me at all sometimes, and that made my stomach tighten in frustration. I couldn't help but wonder if he cared about my thoughts at all.

Without another word, Elimelek turned and called for Mahlon and the servants who were carrying the gifts for the king. With the servants following behind, they began their brief journey down the hill and toward the caravan.

I didn't move from where I stood as I anxiously watched the men reach the edges of the caravan. I involuntarily gasped as the armed men on horseback barreled toward them with weapons drawn, but then sighed in relief when they drew up just short and confronted Elimelek and Mahlon. After what seemed an eternity, finally the men on horseback parted and allowed my men to pass through. They were met on the other side by one man who bowed before he led them to the only tent that had been erected so far. When they disappeared inside, I prayed for their safety, then I turned to double-check on how the preparations were coming.

Several hours passed. I waited on a woven mat on the floor in the cool shade offered within the walls of the new home Elimelek had built. Kilion reclined across the room, resting after completing the work his father had left for him in the primary field: plowing rows for planting. As he rested, his dark face shaded even darker with sunburn and heat, I worked on weaving another floor mat to be used by one of my sons under their bedroll. I hummed songs of hope and praise my mother had taught me when I was a girl while I worked. As I hummed, I tried not to notice the lengthening of the shadows as my husband and eldest still had not returned. I fought the urge to return to the edge of the hill to see if something was happening. I trusted they would return to me, but I was impatient for that return.

Finally, just as I was setting aside the mat to finish later, a tall shadow grew in the doorway.

"Naomi! Naomi! Where are you?" called Elimelek from just outside.

"In here," I called as I rose to my feet.

Elimelek rushed inside, his face flushed with excitement. "Let me tell you! King Eglon has been so gracious!"

I smiled at his excitement, but before he could explain, I interrupted. "How much food do I need to prepare, my love?"

Elimelek stopped short and then laughed. "None, my dear. None. King Eglon has asked that we join him tomorrow evening for a meal with him, his wives, and his younger daughters. Then the day after, he wishes to meet with me regarding this land and our intentions."

I frowned. "Couldn't that be discussed during our meal with him tomorrow?"

"No, my love. No. He is not here for us alone. He's here mainly because one of his daughters is marrying one of the sheik's sons. The sheik's caravan is camped around the river bend. Tomorrow is the wedding feast, and we have been invited to be part of the celebration."

I got caught up in Elimelek's enthusiasm. Of course, it would be a great honor to attend a royal wedding. I tried not to think about how a Moabite wedding might differ from a Hebrew wedding. Just as I thought that,

Mahlon walked into the room and moved to where Kilion still reclined at rest though he was awake and paying close attention to the exchange between us.

Mahlon plopped down beside his younger brother. "Oh, Kilion. The girls! King Eglon's daughters. The nobles' daughters! So many beautiful women…"

I spun on my heel and stared down at my sons, both well past marrying age, but I did not care. "Absolutely not! There were eligible young women for you both to marry at home. And neither of you wanted any part of them. I don't care how long we're among these people, you will not even consider taking a Moabite as a wife."

Kilion rolled his eyes and objected, "Ima, of course we didn't want to marry while we were in Ephrathah. Take a wife just to watch her struggle with childbirth? Watch her wring her hands like you did over every single grain we didn't have? Watch her beg and plead with Yahweh for rain? That is no life for a new couple, a new family."

Stepping back, I stared at my sons. I should have known they would have been aware of the efforts we both had made to feed them. Watching me had caused my sons to lose hope, to put their own lives on hold. Still, just because they were stronger now, and things were better, I could not allow my boys to entertain the idea of marrying Moabites.

Elimelek laid a hand on my shoulder, and I stopped, my eyes still on my sons. "Surely you agree with me: they can't marry Moabite women, Elimelek?"

I did not turn to look at him, but when he cleared his throat, my heart sank, and I dropped my eyes to the ground as I whispered, "Has this come up with the king?"

Elimelek said nothing, but out of the corner of my eye, I saw Mahlon nod his head at Kilion.

"No," I mumbled, but then more loudly, "No! If our boys take Moabite wives, we can never go home. They can never go home! Their wives will never be accepted. They will face ridicule, be cast out, and be reduced in status there. No! You do all this work here just to make them beggars and outcasts there?"

I turned to my husband and gripped his halug in my fists as I pleaded with him. "Husband, please, do not. Do not allow arrangements to be made..."

Elimelek pulled my hands off his halug and held them firmly in his. He stared down at me, and I stared back, trying to fathom what I was seeing in his eyes.

"Naomi, having our sons marry Moabite women will cement our standing here. We cannot count on ever being able to return to Ephrathah. You know that. Our sons will not suffer loneliness here in a land of plenty just to save face in case we can go back."

I flushed under his stare. Doubt and anger filled me. I struggled to keep my emotions under control. Tears of frustration filled my eyes, and I could not bring myself to hold my husband's steely gaze. He had once again made up his mind, and there was no swaying him from it.

I pulled my hands from his grasp. Not willing to look at my sons, I slipped past Elimelek and moved up to the room we shared. I drew the curtain shut across the doorway, certain he would allow me to have some space, and I fell to my knees. Gripping my robes tight to my face to muffle my sobs, I leaned until my forehead touched the floor. I sobbed uncontrollably, allowing my fears, frustrations, and doubts to overwhelm me.

Lord. Lord. Where are you? Please don't allow this to happen. Please, Lord, call us home.

FOUR

I gripped Elimelek's arm tightly but otherwise gave no outward indication I was uncomfortable with the revelry we were part of. King Eglon and his wives had welcomed us with ostentatious enthusiasm and quickly drew us into various conversations as the celebration began.

I couldn't help but stare at the display of wealth surrounding me. The large tent had been laid out richly with colorful rugs, thick blankets, and plush cushions and pillows. Low wooden tables were scattered around an elaborately woven rug with intricate patterns and designs where the new bride and groom were to be wed. Vestiges of the Moabite god were set about the tent and well illuminated with candles and spicy incense. The strong incense and even stronger perfumes made the air in the tent heavy. I resisted the urge to lift the hem of my *tichel* to cover my nose.

I dropped my eyes quickly and stared at the rug I sat on as beautiful young women moved about the tent in wispy clothing that left very little to the imagination. Some carried trays of food, while others kept cups and goblets filled with wine. The rest of the young women moved about singing, chanting, and dancing. I stared at my sons, grimacing inwardly to see their eyes light up as the alluring dancers swayed to the music, moving their bodies seductively about the tent.

My cheeks burned with embarrassment, and I regretted agreeing to attend. More-so, I hated that I agreed to let our sons be present among such debauchery. But I had agreed, so I forced my disgust down and tried to make the best of it. I was determined to be supportive of Elimelek even if we disagreed on the value of this relationship with the Moabite king. As uncomfortable as I was knowing I could not watch the dancers without frowning, I focused my gaze on the intricately woven rug and tried to maintain a slight, albeit fake, smile.

As the evening wore on, Elimelek, deep in conversation with the king and one of his advisers, nudged me, encouraging me to pay attention to what King Eglon's advisor, Bahio, was saying.

"Of course, you must realize we cannot have a foreigner taking land for himself and his family, not even a prestigious man such as yourself." The man paused, and I glanced at him, seeing his smirk widen as he continued, "We are aware of your family's standing in Ephrathah. Despite the difficulties of your hometown, the city, leadership, and news from there are well-known to us. So you can understand why we are a little, shall I say, *concerned* about the precedent it may set for others of your people to just come into our land and claim what is not rightfully theirs to take," said the advisor in his deep voice.

Watching the man, I suspected he was a powerful official among his people. It was likely he held more sway over the Moabites than King Eglon did for the king seemed to simply agree with everything the older man said. Sure enough, King Eglon nodded in agreement with his advisor and leaned forward to add his own thoughts. "Yes. Yes. So, you see, my new friend, I must give you my blessing in order for you to remain among us."

Elimelek scratched his beard. "I understand. I thank you for your gracious..."

The king leaned back and laughed loudly, causing many of the others around the tent to pause in their revelry as they looked his direction, questions in their eyes as their glance took us in as well. "Ah, you Israelites. You're all so humorous. You all sincerely believe you can just go about and do whatever you like —wherever you like."

The king suddenly grew serious, a stern expression on his face. I felt Elimelek's body grow tense beside me. King Eglon narrowed his gaze and leaned in to speak. "No. No. You misunderstand, Elimelek the *Ephrathite*. You need my blessing. I have not given it."

Elimelek started to protest, but King Eglon raised a hand to quiet him. "Wait. Please. I have not given it...," he paused and took a long drink of wine before he continued, "... yet."

He paused for effect, looking at Elimelek closely, then he continued, "Before I bestow my blessing on anyone, particularly a Judean, I wish to learn more about them. I wish to learn more about you, your sons, your wife. I wish to know what you are really doing in my country. Among my people. You have been here just over a month, so my people tell me. Already you have built a permanent home. You are plowing fields. You are setting up stone walls to shelter your herds. Yet despite the obvious signs of an extended stay, you have told my people that you have no intention of remaining."

Elimelek nodded, but Eglon raised his hand again to stop him. "Among your people, there is a law about lying, is there not?"

Elimelek cleared his throat, clearly uneasy with the direction of the conversation. "My Lord, if you will allow me to explain..."

The king leaned back against his cushions as he drank from his wine cup and nodded for Elimelek to continue.

"We left our own home because of the severe famine there. There's nothing left there for us. Maybe, some-day, we could return to the home of our birth, but the famine has stretched on for so long already, and I imagine it will continue to stretch on for many more years. I could not wait any longer. My sons..." he waved at Mahlon and Kilion, "These incredible young men you see before you deserve a better life, a better legacy. We came here initially, yes, just to live among your people in peace for a short while. Still, since we have come, we couldn't help but see how fertile, blessed, and beautiful the land is here. I didn't know I needed your blessing before choosing to remain. Now that I know, I understand, and I hope we'll gain both your trust and your blessing."

Elimelek waited for King Eglon to reply. I resumed staring at the rug as my emotions battled within me once again. Suddenly the king laughed, his laugh washing over me like cold spring water. Chills ran down my spine.

"Oh, Elimelek, have you got the blessing from your wife? Look at her! Look how she glares at the rug!"

I forced myself to remain staring at the rug. I was afraid to look at the king and cause offense because there was no way I could keep my loathing for him off my face.

Elimelek reached out to me and stroked my arm as he responded to the king. "Leaving the home of her birth, her family, and friends was very hard for her, but I assure you, my wife is joined with me in hoping for your gracious permission."

I lifted my gaze just a fraction, and I watched King Eglon stare at Elimelek for a moment without saying a word before he leaned to the side and whispered something in Bahio's ear. The two whispered back and forth, anything that could have been overheard lost in the celebration's commotion that had resumed all around us.

After several minutes, the king leaned toward Elimelek and smiled widely. "I will think on it tonight. Tomorrow, when I come to see all you have done in such a short time, I will give you my answer. What say you?"

Elimelek pulled his hand from my arm, relaxed, and nodded. "Very well. Thank you, my lord."

I tensed at his dismissive response to the king. I knew what he was thinking, and I feared his pride, being of God's chosen people, would anger the king. I tilted my head and glanced at the king. The irritation that flashed across his face both gave me hope and terrified me. Our lives were in that man's hands, and even if Elimelek felt the king owed him some sort of recompense, it was clear the king did not feel the same. He could send us packing, and I would rejoice at that decision. But he could also condemn us to death. Chills ran down my spine.

Returning my stare back to the ornate rug, I started desperately praying to Yahweh for King Eglon to withhold his blessing, and to send us away. Maybe that would finally force Elimelek to see the need for our family to return to Ephrathah.

FIVE

The following morning, I rose early to have all the servants begin preparations. They were busy cleaning, preparing food, setting up more shaded areas for the men to sit and talk, and other areas for the women and children to gather though I wasn't certain the women were going to join the king and his advisors as they visited. Several of the servants reported seeing the king's caravan packing up, and some carts were already leaving with portions of the armed men as well. It seemed the women were moving on ahead of the king. Still, I wanted to be prepared for the entire party.

As the morning passed and the sun rose higher in the sky, one servant saw the king's procession moving up the hill toward us. Elimelek went out to meet them. I remained inside and stood in the door's shadow watching as the group of men, indeed no women among them, approached. The men paid me no attention as they wandered around the house with its ground floor barn and a common area where we shared our meals. Then they moved to the sleeping area upstairs before they moved into the dusty yard, the small herb garden, and then along to the newly plowed and planted fields and fenced corrals for the small herds of goats and sheep.

After a while, the men finally returned, all appearing to be in good spirits. They talked amongst themselves as though they were the oldest of friends. I watched Elimelek lead them all to a large tent we had set up that offered shade while also allowing for the brisk breeze to move through and cool them.

Immediately, I sent my maidservants to the tent to give the men refreshments. I watched carefully to make sure none of our guests took liberties with my serving girls, but I made no attempt to join the men. Elimelek had made it abundantly clear that I was not welcome to be part of whatever proposition the king laid out. After the king observed my sour disposition, Elimelek expressed, with no room for argument, that he did not want my presence to risk the king's approval and permission to remain.

Grudgingly but trying to be obedient, I remained in the house. Not that I wanted to be there in the tent with people I didn't trust, I was curious what was being decided without me. I watched from the doorway or from the window, while I also helped put food on the trays to be carried to the tent. I heard the men talking, the flow of their voices rising and falling away, sometimes rising even louder as someone laughed or as the conversation took an animated turn.

Food went to the tent. Empty trays returned.

Drinks went to the tent. Empty casks returned.

In a single meal, I found nearly half our food and wine stores had been used up, and we were not yet harvesting. I stared about at what was left of our stores and wrung my hands nervously. I tried to ration out in my mind what we still had and what it would take to remain until harvest or to return to Ephrathah. If we left for Ephrathah, I was certain what we had left would last us for the journey was shorter than the time until harvest. If we stayed, we would have to rely on bartering and trading to get us through till harvest. As more laughter echoed in my ears and another cask of wine left our house to go to the tent, I sighed internally.

When another servant returned to get another cask, I stopped the girl. Together, we poured the wine into three empty casks and then filled them the rest of the way with water. I carefully swished the wine and water mixture to mix them well. As I did so, I bid the girl not to say anything to our guests. Then I sent her back to the tent with one cask and set the other two near the door to be taken first. I prayed none of the men would notice the wine had been watered down. But shortly after, Elimelek walked in with an empty cask in his hands.

"Is this wine different?" he asked.

I pulled him to the back of the room where it was coolest and where the remaining wine was stored. I waved my hands at the three remaining casks.

"I had to water it down, my love. We need what is left to get us through to harvest," I explained.

Elimelek stared at the little that was left. "Surely we didn't drink so much!"

I stared at him in disbelief. He was there in the tent full of men, and he was oblivious to the amount of food and wine being passed around? "You're not drunk, husband, but how many of the men in that tent are?"

Elimelek shook his head and sighed. "Most of them."

He laid the empty cask at my feet. "Okay, I'll inform the king that we are out of wine. I can only guess what he will say. He has high expectations of everyone around him."

I reached out and touched Elimelek's arm, afraid to ask the question that was nagging at my thoughts. "Are we staying? Has he granted us his blessing?"

Elimelek nodded but frowned. His brows knit together tightly as he avoided meeting my gaze. "Yes. But with conditions."

"Conditions?"

"Yes. I'll tell you later. He wants me to visit him in Kir-Moab, at his palace."

I couldn't help the way my mouth opened in surprise nor the blurted question. My voice raised in sudden panic. "What? When? Just you? Or all of us?"

Elimelek kissed me on the forehead, ignoring the pitch of my questions. "You, me, and our sons."

I felt myself deflate, but I nodded. "I see. Okay. Well, you can tell me later. You shouldn't leave them for too long."

Elimelek smiled at me, but there was a reserved quality to his smile, and I knew that whatever the proposition was, I was not likely to be happy about it. Without another word on the subject, Elimelek left me standing in the back of the room while he rejoined the king and his men.

The king remained for another hour before calling his advisors together and announcing it was time they moved on to meet the caravan wherever it had set up for the night. Elimelek ushered them to the base of the hill where their horses waited. By the time they left and Elimelek rejoined me at the top of the hill, the day was entirely spent.

We watched the king's party disappear and went to the house. As we got near, Elimelek moved past me and up the stairs. I turned and followed him in silence. He entered our sleeping area, and I stood waiting for him to tell me all that was said. However, he laid down on our wide mat without a word, his back to me, and before I could utter a word, he began snoring.

Disappointed and irritated, I returned to the main floor where Terah and the other servants were cleaning and putting things away. I helped them for a while, but the questions burning in my mind started pounding around in my skull, and I feared I would lash out. I dismissed the servants for the night and worked quietly on my own, trying to keep my thoughts from going in a hundred different directions. After a while, I wandered out to the largest tent that was still standing. As I neared it, I heard my sons talking in low voices inside.

I slipped inside and allowed my eyes to adjust to the lights of the oil lanterns. Seeing me, my sons rose to their feet. They greeted me with warm hugs. I sat down with them, allowing myself to relax my arms and legs for the first time all day.

"How did it go?" I asked.

Mahlon glanced at Kilion with a worried look. "*Abba* asked us not to say anything yet. He wants us all to talk about it in the morning."

Kilion nodded in agreement. "It's okay, Ima. I promise. It's nothing bad."

I smiled weakly, knowingly. "If it were nothing bad, my son, your father wouldn't ask you not to talk about it."

In response, they turned their gazes downward and said nothing more. Realizing I would learn nothing from them, tension instantly tightening my chest and neck, I got to my feet. I felt their eyes on me and knew they were concerned. They were not accustomed to keeping secrets from me. I turned back to them and watched emotions play across their faces. Anger flared within me. How dare Elimelek ask our sons to keep a secret from me! One that he had to sleep on? We never kept things from each other. That wasn't how our marriage worked. That wasn't how our family worked.

I leaned over each of my sons and kissed them on the forehead, mumbling good night to each of them, then I turned and left the tent. I wandered to the edge of the hill and stared out into the night for a long time. Doubts, frustrations, and fears battled in my mind leaving my thoughts a muddled mess. Finally, after what felt like an eternity, my body and mind grew weary. I returned to our room, where I laid down beside Elimelek. As sleep overtook me, my mind still troubled, my prayers were pleas of frustration, sadness, and worry.

SIX

I got little rest that night. I got little rest for the week that followed as Elimelek continued to avoid telling me the context of the conversation he had had with the king. The more I pressed, the more distant he became. I tried to pry the secret out of my sons, but they too grew distant. After seven days of not getting answers, I tried to accept that Elimelek would tell me when the timing was right. During the day, I could pretend I wasn't frustrated but at night...

Night was different. My worries gave birth to strangely vivid dreams that verged on nightmares. When I woke a week after the king had visited us, I was shaky with nervousness. Rather than follow my normal morning routine, I knelt beside the thick mat that was my bed. Bowing my head, I tried to pray away the images that had been in my dreams. I tried to pray away the feeling of dread that permeated my mind and knotted my gut. Foreboding threatened to consume me, and my fear of the unknown that lay ahead left me frustrated to the point of silent tears.

After several minutes, unable to put my thoughts to words, unable to utter anything beyond, "Dear Lord," I got angry and gave up. I pushed myself to my feet and shook my head in a futile effort to shake the thoughts away. When that failed as well, I forced myself to start my routine while I hoped that staying busy would help quiet my anxious mind.

After I washed and dressed, my hair braided, the tears washed away, I joined my family for their morning meal. I smiled weakly at the morning greetings from my sons and ignored Elimelek's greeting altogether. I couldn't help noticing how quickly he finished his meal before he left without a word.

"Ima, are you upset with Abba?" Mahlon asked.

I avoided looking at him. I didn't want to burden my boys with my fears and doubts, so I shook my head from side to side. "No, I'm just tired," I told him.

I tried to tell myself I wasn't really upset with my husband. I did not like that he made such important decisions without including me. I did not like the feeling in the pit of my stomach that revolved around things I knew he was keeping from me. There was a lot I was unhappy with at that moment, but angry wasn't how I would have described my feelings.

Mahlon knew better than to push the issue, so he returned his attention to what remained of his meal.

Then he too rose to his feet and left, leaving Kilion alone with me. I seized the opportunity to pry. Kilion was much easier to sway, more eager to please.

"Son, what is the plan for you all today?"

Kilion reached for another piece of flat bread and a handful of dates. While he ate, he responded, "I think Abba wants to start the additions to the house today. Before the rains begin."

I leaned back and looked at Kilion. "This house is big enough. What do we need with additions? Or is he finally going to add on another storeroom for me so this can be our main living space?"

Kilion shook his head. "No. Maybe. I don't know about a storeroom. But since Mahlon and I are getting married..."

He turned beet red.

"Married?" I asked, working hard to keep my voice calm and even. "But there are no Ephrathites here. Does he mean to send to Ephrathah for wives for you both?"

Kilion's face reddened even more, and for a moment, he did not answer.

I leaned in. "It's okay, my son. I want nothing but the best for both of you. You can tell me."

Kilion smiled at me, but I could see his uncertainty. Even though he was a grown man, already in his twenties, I demanded his honesty. No matter what his father said, Kilion could not keep a secret from me.

"King Eglon made Abba an offer. He thinks we are people of great standing in Ephrathah, and he wants to show us kindness by allowing us to stay here among his own people..."

"But...?" I coaxed, impatient for him to get to the point.

"But he thought it would be best if there was a tangible union between our family and his. So Mahlon and I are betrothed to two of his daughters."

I felt the color leave my face. My chest grew tight as though someone was squeezing the air out of me. I stood and began pacing around the room.

As I paced the room, I tried to sort out my thoughts, speaking them out, hoping to make sense of this horrible revelation, "This can't be. We could never return to Ephrathah. We'd be outcast. Marrying Moabites. Bringing their customs and culture into our home. Oh... why? Why would he agree to this?"

I stopped and faced Kilion, who was listening and watching me, his expression unreadable. "Son, when is this supposed to take place? These marriages?"

Kilion, clearly excited, replied, "During our trip to Kir-Moab. Father intends to have the additions finished before we go and hopes to have made some valuable trades before then so we have adequate bridal gifts for the king because he has promised incredible dowries to come along with his daughters."

I couldn't bear to listen to another word. The lump in my chest moved to my throat. My shock and anger threatened to make me explode. I rushed out of the house in search of Elimelek, determined to give him a piece of my mind before it was too late.

～

I rushed out to the fields where I knew Elimelek was directing the men on what he wanted done for the day. As I neared the edge of the fields, I saw him standing with a group of men far across on the other side.

Trembling with anger, I picked my way over the rows of planted seedlings. I worked over the words I wanted to say. Determined, I had to make him understand, to convince him not to continue with the arranged marriages. He was going to listen to me even if it meant he slept on the roof for a month. He was going to listen. He was going to do the right thing for our sons, for our family.

As I drew closer, I saw the way Elimelek was leaning in to address the men, and my determined arguments faded to the back of my mind. I knew that stance. He was aggravated and trying to explain something. The closer I got, the more I realized that he was in the middle of an aggressive discussion with the men, all Moabites hired to help with the farming.

I stopped in shock as one man lashed out at Elimelek, knocking him to the ground. In horror, I watched from the middle of the field as the men surrounded Elimelek while he struggled to get up. I tried to cry out, but my voice came out a mere squeak. I stood frozen in place, watching in dismay as the men beat and kicked at Elimelek.

Suddenly, I unfroze. My shrill cry for help pierced through the air as I started running to help him, not caring about the men.

The Moabites stopped beating Elimelek and stared in my direction. They looked down at Elimelek's still body and spat on him before they left without so much as another glance in my direction. I raced to Elimelek, no longer caring about where I stepped as I ran. After what felt like an eternity, I reached him and flung myself down on the ground at his side.

"Elimelek!" I cried, but he did not respond. "Oh, Lord, please, no!"

Elimelek's face was already swollen. His eyes were black; his nose was broken and bleeding. Both his lips were cut, bleeding, and severely swollen. Blood ran from cuts on his cheeks, in his hairline, down his neck, and along his collarbone. I gently cradled his head, afraid to move him. As I did so, fluid ran out from his ears and dread nearly overwhelmed me. I'd seen violence such as this before; I knew enough to know that it would take a long time for him to recover from his injuries if he could recover from them at all. He let out a ragged breath as I wiped his face with my shawl.

"My love?" I whispered, but he remained unconscious.

Sitting there on the ground, I looked all around me. Where were our servants? Where was Mahlon? I looked all back the way I had come and finally saw a group of people coming from the direction of the house. Carefully, I laid Elimelek's head on my shawl on the ground. I stood up and frantically waved.

At first, it appeared no one saw me, but then figures broke away from the group, and some ran toward me. Realizing help was on the way, I let my body sink back to my knees as tears flooded my eyes. I leaned forward and rested my head on his chest, listening to his weak heartbeat and his labored breathing. As the tears ran freely, I begged God to show him healing mercies.

Suddenly, powerful arms wrapped around me and voices cried out, asking what had happened. I heard Mahlon shout for order and then his calm voice directing the servants to carry his father back home. The warm arms that were around me lifted me to my feet, but my legs had no strength, so they lifted me from the ground. I found myself in Mahlon's arms as he carried me back toward the house. Safe in his arms, even though worry consumed me, I closed my eyes and prayed over and over for everything to be okay.

After several long minutes, I realized we were near the house. "Wait," I whispered, my voice tiny and scared. Mahlon stopped. "I will walk from here, son."

Mahlon nodded and gently put me down, his eyes wide with concern. I steadied myself by hanging on to his arm with one hand while I wiped my face with the sleeve of my robe.

"Ima, what happened? Did you see?" His hand lifted my chin gently, and his eyes searched my face.

I nodded, unable to meet his stare. "It was those men," I replied, hearing the deep bitterness in my voice. "I told him they couldn't be trusted..."

"What men?"

I looked up at Mahlon. New anger flared up and I trembled with new rage, my husband's agreement with the king momentarily forgotten. "Those godforsaken Moabites he hired."

Mahlon's eyes expressed his surprise. "Surely not. Those men were recommended..."

"...by the king," I finished. "Yes. I know. Men we could trust, he told your father."

"Ima, are you sure?"

I nodded. "They attacked him and beat him right in front of me. Then they just walked away like it was no big deal, like they knew nothing would happen to them for what they did."

Mahlon sighed deeply. He started to say something but stopped as loud voices were suddenly heard from somewhere by the house.

I forced my anger down and squeezed his arm. "Come! We have to tend to your father's wounds."

Mahlon nodded and walked quietly beside me in silence. I could feel the tension in his arm, and the set to his jaw told me he was trying to think.

Together, we reached the house and rushed inside to find Kilion and the servants gathered around the table where the men had laid Elimelek to be tended to. I rushed to his side as I called out orders for clean cloths, hot water, and specific herbs. While I waited for the items to be brought to me, I leaned down and listened to his breathing. It was even fainter now. A chill ran through my body, and I shuddered. I could not lose him. Not in this foreign land. Not when we were clearly surrounded by enemies.

I stood back up and motioned for Mahlon and Kilion to help me undress their father. Once his clothes were removed, the extent of the attack was revealed.

His body was covered in shallow cuts and deep bruises. It was obvious just from looking that his ribs had been broken in several places. I gasped at the blood pooling at his side, from an inexplicable gash. Had someone actually stabbed him? Deep dread filled me as I realized only God could heal him now. But God had not shown us any mercy as of late. My anger turned to an even deeper bitterness, and despair threatened to overwhelm me.

Why, Lord? Is this our punishment? Is this my punishment? But you know how I have tried! You know how I have begged and pleaded with him to remain faithful to you. Now you punish not just him but me and my sons as well? Lord, why?

Heaviness settled in my gut.

Finally, the supplies I asked for were set before me. I set about washing away the blood, working to sew up the cuts, applying herb poultices to the cuts and bruises. As I worked, I watched for any reaction, anything to signify he could feel me working on his wounds, but he remained unresponsive throughout all my ministrations. Once I had done all I could do, I covered his naked body.

Exhausted, I sank to a stool that sat by the table and was suddenly aware that I was the only person left in the room with Elimelek. I reached for his hand.

"You infuriating man!" I said in a low voice. "You can't leave me here. Wake up, and fight to get better! You can't..." My voice cracked as I stared at his broken face, very little resemblance there to the man who I knew to be so handsome, stubborn, and strong. "You can't leave me. Please, my love, don't leave me."

I laid my head on his chest. If he died, what then? He'd leave us stranded in this godforsaken land at the mercy of a duplicitous king. What would become of our sons? What would become of me? Would the Moabites allow us to remain? Would they kill us? Worse, what if they captured us as slaves? Without Elimelek, we'd be without our family leader, without the prestige of his position. Would King Eglon renegotiate with Mahlon? How did Moabites handle contracts when one half of the party died?

My body shook and trembled as the thoughts rushed through my mind. Every worst-case scenario played out in vivid detail, raising the hair on my arms and making my heart race. I gripped his hand, my face still pressed to his chest, and as anxiety and fear built, I wept.

SEVEN

For three days, I sat with Elimelek. They seemed to stretch on with no end as I tenderly cared for his deep wounds. As I begged and pleaded with God, I forced water down Elimelek's throat. I threatened him, then I pleaded with him despite knowing he could not hear me. Through it all, I refused to leave his side. I barely ate or drank, and I certainly didn't sleep except in tiny snatches when my body refused to function any longer. Our sons sat with us on and off, but they knew there was work to be done, so they took over their father's responsibilities. They did their best to keep the work in the fields and on the house moving forward despite the loss of the Moabite workers.

Mahlon told me he sent word to the king reporting what had happened. He told me he wasn't sure what he expected, but he hoped the king did not know that the men he had recommended were so treacherous. Part of him, he said, hoped the king would send help, but he could not fathom what kind of help that might be.

Kilion also expressed hope that help would be sent. Yet the days passed, and no word returned. Both of the young men's hopes were in vain. I was not surprised.

Late in the evening of the third day, I watched Elimelek take his last shallow breath. I was numb. All my emotions spent, I reached my hand to his neck and felt for a pulse. Confirming that there was no pulse and no breath, I sat staring at the broken body before me. I wanted to be angry or sad. Anything! But I was left with nothing. Dry and hollow, I slowly stood and pulled the blanket up over his face. I leaned forward and kissed his face through the blanket, then I walked out of the house and approached the large fire where our sons and all the servants sat eating their evening meal.

Kilion saw me first. Laying his food on the ground, he rushed to my side. "Abba is...?"

I merely stared at him, trying to form the words I dreaded to hear spoken out loud. Kilion did not wait for a response. He rushed into the house, followed closely by Mahlon. I heard their cries of dismay, but I still felt nothing. I sat on a low stool by the fire and reached out to Terah, who silently handed me a clay bowl with some stewed meat and herbs. No one said anything to me. They simply sat in silence around the fire and watched me pick at my meal. After several long minutes, Mahlon and Kilion returned to the fire, emotions playing across their faces, but neither said a word to each other or to me.

Once I finished eating, and after a long collective silence around the fire, Mahlon cleared his throat.

"Ima, what do we do now?" he asked, his voice barely above a whisper.

I looked at him. Could he not see how empty I was? Could he not fathom the depths of my despair, or how truly lost I felt without Elimelek to make every decision? The last thing I wanted to think of was what to do next. Not for now. Not for tomorrow. I fought against the impatience I felt, but I knew I had to tell him something. "Not now, son. We will discuss it after your father is buried."

"But..."

My stomach knotted. I gripped the rope tied around my waist, willing my sudden anger down. I clenched my teeth, biting back harsh words, as I raised a hand to stop his persistence.

"I said, not now."

Unable to withstand any more conversation or questions, I handed the nearly untouched bowl back to Terah and returned to the house, leaving Mahlon and Kilion to discuss among themselves what our future might hold.

Several days later, still lost on how to proceed with Elimelek gone, I deeply regretted not talking to

Mahlon the night Elimelek died. Had I answered him right then, maybe my eldest would have been more open to my suggestion. My heart screamed to return to the home of our birth, but I didn't. Now every time I brought up going back to Ephrathah, both my sons argued against it. In reality, the decision really fell on Mahlon's shoulders now that he was the head of our family. I buckled under the sudden change in the family dynamic. When Elimelek was alive, I still held maternal power over my sons. They heeded me as they would have their father, but now that he was gone, both young men were finding they could spread their wings.

In the middle of my chaotic thoughts and grief over not just my husband but also a missed opportunity, Mahlon approached me once again. "Ima, what do you think?"

I jumped at his intrusion and looked up at him. "Hmmm? What?"

Mahlon took a seat on the ground next to me as I pressed my hands into a bowl of dough, kneading it for our bread.

"Kilion and I have been discussing our options. One is to return to Ephrathah as you have suggested, but," he hesitated, "we have had word about the famine there. Rumor carried by the caravans is that the famine is worse than ever. The other option is to stay here where we know the land could yield a decent harvest."

I started to protest, but Mahlon continued quickly, "We know you long for home, Ima, but now that I'm the head of the house, I think I understand why Abba was so determined to stay. It's my responsibility now to take care of you and Kilion. I know Kilion may not be with us much longer. I think he is ready to head out on his own, but until that happens, I still need to think of what is best for all of us."

I felt my head droop as defeat washed over me. I did not want to argue with my son as I had with my husband.

After several long minutes of silence passed between us, Mahlon reached out and touched me gently on the hand. "Also, we have had word from the king. He wishes for us to keep our plans, but instead of next week, out of respect for Abba, the king asks us to visit in a couple of weeks."

I looked up quickly and stared at Mahlon, my eyes wide in anger and shock at the suggestion. "They were his men, Mahlon," anger seething through my teeth as I spoke. "The men he sent us to work the fields with you and your father. You can't really think I'm going to visit the home of the man who may have been the reason your father is no longer with us."

Mahlon flushed, and he clenched his jaw. Finally, he replied, "Ima, we are going. He is the king of this land, and not going could incite more action against us if he was behind the attack in the first place. We must go.

We will go. And... we will stay here so long as he, the king, allows us to."

Without another word, Mahlon rose to his feet and strode off toward the fields. I watched my eldest walk away and felt pride and anger battle within me. There he was... truly a man, making decisions the way he thought best, but just as with my husband, I couldn't shake the feeling of dread that had sat in the pit of my stomach from the day we left Ephrathah.

Carefully, I set the bowl of dough aside and bowed my head as I lifted my hands to the sky.

Please work in my son. Please, Yahweh, lead us home.

I spent several more minutes in prayer and thought, praying for the powerful emotions within me to subside. But the more I thought, the more unsettled I became. Finally, I sighed in frustration.

Are you even listening anymore?

The silence in my mind and the hollowness in my heart convinced me Yahweh was no longer concerned with the affairs of my family.

EIGHT

Two weeks later, I tried not to let anxiety and mistrust show on my face as Kilion led me before the king's throne. Mahlon had already approached the king, bowed, and recited the courtesies that had been shared with us by the king's advisor that morning. My eldest stood to the side, tall and proud, with a small smile plastered on his face. I cast a sideways glance at Kilion and saw he wore the same small smile.

In that instant, I knew both my sons were afraid of the king before them. I forced my gaze back to the man on the throne and saw cunning and malice in his eyes, looks I might have noticed the first time in his presence had I not stared at the ground the entire time. My heart jumped into my throat, but rather than run away as my instincts warned me to do, I let Kilion lead me closer to the lion in front of me.

When we reached the base of the raised throne, Kilion gently pulled me down beside him. Together we prostrated ourselves before the king. I remained prostrate on the floor as taught by the advisor while Kilion raised himself to his knees and recited his greeting to the king. I didn't hear a word of it as I screamed internally that we shouldn't be here. After what seemed like an eternity with my forehead pressed to the cold stone floor, I felt Kilion gently pull at my arm, and I got to my feet. As I stood back up, I watched the king. His mouth was moving, but again, I couldn't seem to hear the words for the internal fight inside me. In a daze, I allowed Kilion to turn me to the side and lead me to where Mahlon stood.

After several long minutes, I realized others were being presented to the king as well. My breathing started slowing, my head started clearing, and I looked around the large room. I started really seeing the king and his throne.

King Eglon was an impressive man in his colorful robes with his gems and jewelry of silver and gold. Behind him stood one of his wives, his first wife, mother to the king's only male heir. On the other side stood the advisor, Bahio, who had instructed us of protocol when approaching the king.

Opposite of where I stood, women of all ages sat on rugs, leaning against plush pillows. The women ranged in age from their teens to ages nearer my own. Several had small children sitting with them. I realized I was looking at the king's harem—his wives and children. It occurred to me that the young women my sons were to marry were probably among those women, so I scoured the faces of the women.

Which ones were they?

While I examined the women across from me, my thoughts drifted to the past few days. Prior to leaving for our visit with King Eglon, I had pleaded with Mahlon to turn down the king's demands for him and Kilion to continue with the arranged marriages. Mahlon had been kind enough to listen to my fears and doubts and my reminder that if they married the King's daughters, then they could not return to Ephrathah.

Kilion had not been so kind. After his father's murder, Kilion turned from a gentle and sensitive young man into one I no longer recognized. He had become cold, hard, dismissive, and abrupt. In him, I saw a harsher reflection of everything I was feeling. He dismissed my concerns before I finished expressing them, leaving me to finish my pleading with his older brother.

In the end, Mahlon also dismissed my concerns, and we had begun our journey to the king's palace.

I paid no attention to the other people presenting themselves to King Eglon until Mahlon gripped my hand and caught my attention. I looked at him, and he nodded toward the entrance to the throne room. I leaned forward a little to see past the people who now stood between me and the door.

In the doorway stood two young women with gauzy veils over their faces. Both women were dressed in pale gowns that swept the floor and wore necklaces, bracelets, anklets, and rings that tinkled and rang as they walked toward the throne.

King Eglon rose to his feet. His expression changed to one of pride and even warmth as he stepped to the bottom of the dais to meet the young women. Both women bowed before him, but he stopped them before they prostrated themselves before him. He raised their veils one by one and kissed them gently on their cheeks before he turned them to face the audience.

"My people! I am honored to present to you my two beautiful daughters, Orpah and Ruth. Today is a day of days! Today, my precious daughters are to be wed to princes of Ephrathah."

I glanced up at Mahlon, who turned red in embarrassment at the obvious mistake regarding our standing among Ephrathites.

King Eglon waved for Mahlon and Kilion to join him. As my sons stepped away from my side, pieces of my heart were being ripped from my chest even as the room erupted in shouts of joy and celebration. King Eglon took each of my sons by their hands. He led Mahlon first to stand by the daughter he called Ruth, and Kilion to the daughter he called Orpah. I stared at the couples and forced myself to really see the young women, the half-sisters, who were about to become part of our family.

Orpah was truly the more striking of the two. She was nearly as tall as Kilion with beautiful thick brown hair that had gold and silver spun into her tight braids. She had huge brown eyes fringed with thick black lashes, a little upturned nose, and a full mouth with red tinted lips. She was darkly tanned and slender but curvy in all the right places, her long legs noticeable through the slits in her gown. From the way she looked around, she knew she was beautiful. I noticed the lift of her chin and the set of her shoulders. Orpah was a proud young woman.

Ruth, on the other hand, while quite pretty was not equal to her sister. Ruth stood nearly a head shorter than Orpah. Her hair, also brown, was not as thick nor as lustrous, but her eyes were a deep green with a fringe of thick long lashes, her most beautiful feature. Her nose was a little long for her face, and her mouth was a little small, which made it look like she was perpetually pouting. The red tint to her thin lips made her look even more pale since her skin was not near as dark as her sister's. While she was not beautiful or proud like Orpah, there was a confidence in her that showed in the way she stood and made eye contact with the surrounding people rather than looking down her nose at them. I noted too that Ruth's gown, jewelry, and gems were more exquisite than those of her sister, a testament to the fact that Ruth was the eldest of the two and why she was paired with Mahlon.

King Eglon looked from one daughter to the next, his back now to the audience, but easy for me to see from where I stood. He clearly loved both of his daughters. Noting that affection touched me more deeply that I expected. *Maybe these unions would not be so bad after all.* I cringed inwardly at my concession, but a tiny voice inside me reminded me that the young women were at the mercy of their father as much as my family. Keeping that in mind, I made up my mind to do my best to love the young women as if they were my own daughters.

King Eglon took one of Ruth's hands and put it in one of Mahlon's, then he did the same with Orpah and Kilion. Then with one of his hands on each of their grasping hands, he raised his head to the idol that stood behind his throne. He called out a prayer to *Chemosh* to bless the union of both couples. As soon as he began his prayer, everyone in the throne room fell to their knees and bowed before the idol, the king, and the young couples.

I stared around in sudden fear. I would not pray to their god.

Instead, I bowed my head and began praying earnestly for protection for my sons. Would my refusal to join everyone else cause my sons harm? I stood, shaking in dread and fear, while King Eglon continued his prayer.

After he finished his prayer and turned back to the throne, he seemed to see right through me. I breathed a deep sigh of relief when he failed to react to my obvious affront. In a daze, I realized my own prayer had been answered in a miraculous manner.

"Thank you, Lord," I whispered into the air.

King Eglon raised his arms to the crowd of people in the room. "Before Chemosh, these young people have been joined in marriage. Further, they have gained my blessing. Join me, my daughters, and now my sons, as we celebrate their union!"

As he lowered his arms, the people erupted in more cheers and clapping, and musicians at the back of the room began playing increasingly wild music so different from the gentle strumming on lutes or the haunting tones of flutes my people were known for. The king returned to his throne, leaving both young couples standing awkwardly before him, unsure of how to proceed. Seeing the couples floundering, I stepped forward to them. These were still my sons, and now these were also my daughters.

I approached Kilion and Orpah first. Kilion and Orpah both stiffened at my approach. Still, I hugged and kissed my son gently. "My blessings on you, my son. I pray you and your beautiful bride find love and unity."

Kilion met my gaze, and he relaxed visibly. "Thank you, Ima."

He glanced at the young woman at his side, her hand still in his, and I could tell he wondered at his luck. I'm sure he felt like he had just won one over his brother despite being the younger one. He confirmed my suspicion when he glanced at Mahlon and smiled smugly, but his brother didn't appear to get the unspoken jibe.

He shrugged his shoulders and returned his attention to his new bride.

I saw Kilion's smug smile aimed at his brother but ignored it and turned to Orpah. I took the young woman's hands in mine. "Welcome to my family, Orpah. I pray you find warmth and comfort with me and deep abiding love with my son."

Orpah's gaze was cool and aloof as she responded. The smile she gave me was touched by a cruel smirk. "I guess Father didn't tell you. Kilion and I will be remaining here in the city. Your prayers need to be that your sweet son finds those things here with my family."

I stiffened and glanced past Orpah to where King Eglon sat, observing my interaction with keen interest. I smiled weakly then looked at Kilion. "Did you know this?"

Kilion shrugged. "It was mentioned when Abba was still alive. It's okay; I have been talking with Mahlon about it, and we are agreed. This is a fantastic opportunity for our family."

I felt as though a knife had been slid into my ribs, but I forced my smile to remain in place. "Very well. Then I wish you both happiness in your new beginning."

I moved over to Mahlon and Ruth. "Why didn't you tell me Kilion was going to remain here?" I accused, forgoing my blessing on Mahlon and Ruth's marriage.

Mahlon flushed and looked away, instead letting his gaze wander around the room as if he were worried anyone would overhear our exchange. "I would rather not talk about it here, Ima."

I leaned in and whispered harshly, "It appears you had no intention of talking to me about it at all, son."

I was about to say more, but Ruth quickly stepped forward and took my hand. I found myself stopped short, looking into Ruth's deep green eyes, a small smile on the young woman's lips. "Mother... May I call you Mother? Or... is it Ima? The word Mahlon uses? My mother died in childbirth with me. I'm not certain how I should address you."

I started at the blunt openness, but nodded mutely, unsure of the young woman.

"Ima, then...," smiled Ruth warmly, "I'm eager to see my new home with you and Mahlon. Father has told me that your late husband and sons have turned that patch of land into quite the oasis."

I cringed at the mention of Elimelek but nodded in response. "Yes. I guess it is turning into a pretty spot."

Ruth continued by lifting her hands so I could see them. "I'm not used to a great deal of work, but I hope I can learn from you?"

I stared at the young woman's hands, which actually were not as clear and soft as I would have expected of a princess. Instead, I saw cuts and scratches along her palms and a few calluses on the balls of her hands. I glanced at Mahlon; his look of disbelief matched my own. I looked at Ruth in surprise, searching her face for some sign of subterfuge. This young woman seemed to be serious. Yet she was a princess. It was clear she was no stranger to some sort of work, but she expected us to believe she was willing to share the demands of working the land? I stared deeply into Ruth's eyes and found that I believed the girl.

I squeezed Ruth's hands gently. "If you are sincere, then yes, I will be honored and happy to teach you whatever you wish to learn."

I turned back to Mahlon, "Can we talk later?"

Mahlon frowned but nodded.

Nodding in reply, I kissed my eldest son on both cheeks and whispered in his ear, "I sincerely pray that your marriage is one of love and happiness, my son."

Mahlon whispered back, "Me too, Ima."

NINE

The wedding celebrations with King Eglon lasted for five days and nights. I often left the ungodly celebrations, unwilling to partake in or even observe the ways of the Moabites that so obviously clashed with what I had been taught. I cried out in my heart as both my sons and my new daughters were expected to take part in strange rituals and dances that made their union seem a mere suggestion rather than something holy and significant to be cherished.

There were differences in how each of my sons and my new daughters reacted to the revelry. Based on my observations, I realized my sons were matched with women who shared their basic personalities. Where Mahlon was more reserved and withdrawn throughout the celebrations, Kilion embraced the revelry and came alive to it. Same with the young women. Ruth seemed to shy away from being the center of attention; she seemed uncomfortable with it and often moved to the edges to give over to someone who was more happy with it. However, Orpah not only reveled in having all eyes on her, she sought it out, more than once going out of her way to draw attention to herself.

Still, as much as I could observe, most of my days among the king's people were largely spent in his expansive gardens with their high walls, where I was mostly left alone. I could still hear the singing and carousing inside. Now and then, the celebration would spill out even into the gardens, but overall, I found solace among the silent fragrant flowers, tall bushes, and stunted trees. Early on, I discovered a beautifully ornate well in the center of the garden that had a small fountain to the side of it.

Often I sat on the edge of the fountain, many times lost in troubled prayers. I wanted to be happy for my sons. Wasn't it every mother's dream to have her children married well so that they could live better lives, have children of their own to carry on the legacy of their faith and their family? Bitterness welled up inside me as I wished the women chosen for my sons were women of Ephrathah, strong in faith, obedient to Yahweh. That it was not so made me sad for my sons rather than happy.

On our last day among King Eglon's people, I was deep in thought in the garden when the king himself found me and encroached on my solitude.

"My dear, Naomi," he called out to me from across an open area, startling me from my thoughts. I rose to my feet, thankful that he was behind me so I could compose my face before I turned to greet him. When I turned to him, I realized he was not alone. I recognized the older man who was with him though he stood a couple steps behind the king in obvious deference.

I bobbed a curt bow from my waist in order to maintain protocol, but I stared at the king in silence.

He must have sensed my unease, because he waved to a long bench that sat at the edge of the small clearing. "Might we sit and speak together as a father to a mother, and a mother to a father?"

My eyebrows raised in surprise, but I nodded and followed the king and his advisor to the bench. The king motioned for me to have a seat. The man with him sat beside me while the king remained standing before us.

"Naomi, I understand that you have had some misgivings about the marriage of your sons to my daughters..."

I leaned forward to interject, but the king raised a hand to quiet me.

He continued, "I also understand that you believe that I somehow had a hand in the death of your husband."

Sucking in my breath, I bit back a retort. I glanced at the man sitting beside me and shifted uncomfortably at the way he was watching me. I scowled at the stranger then turned to stare back at King Eglon. He stood in front of me, his hands clasped in front of him. The way he stared down at me, I realized he was intent on putting me in my place. I felt chills pass up and down my spine, and internally, I cried out to God: *Lord, please protect me from this man.*

King Eglon smirked at me as though able to read my silent prayer. "I can assure you I intended no harm to your husband. I can understand your misgivings, and so I am a little surprised that you allowed your sons to still join into this union with my daughters... and with me."

He paused for a moment then glanced at the man next to me. "I want you to meet my trusted emissary. Naomi, this is Mateo. I asked him to come along with me, hoping his presence will offer you some comfort as I assure you I wish only the best for you and your sons now that you have my blessing to remain in Moab among my people. Mateo will accompany you and Mahlon back to your home. I have asked him to be an emissary between your household and mine to make sure you have everything you need."

I fumed inside but responded in an even tone, "You mean you wish him to make sure we do nothing that goes against your wishes."

King Eglon laughed out loud and unveiled malice flashed in his eyes. "That may be exactly so, but I know you are a wise woman. I know you want the best for your sons. With one son remaining with you while the other is safely with me, I know neither of us will have to worry about the other. Am I right?"

I caught the not-so-subtle threat, and I grimaced. After a few seconds of silence, I rose to my feet and nodded to the king. "I think I understand you perfectly."

I bowed, and without waiting to be dismissed, fled the gardens. Once I was safely back in my room, I saw all my belongings had already been packed and removed from the room. A servant waited in the hall and called out to me as I stood staring about the empty room.

"Your son is already at the gate, Mistress. He waits for you there."

I didn't hesitate. The gate out of the palace and away from the godless king was exactly the direction I wanted to be headed. I rushed out the door and with the servant leading the way ran to the gate where Mahlon, Ruth, and Mateo waited for me. It wasn't until we were several hours away that I realized I hadn't even thought to stay long enough to say goodbye to Kilion. Had that been by design? Had the king known his words would upset me to the point of simply leaving my child in my haste to get away?

TEN

The rest of that first year in Moab went by quickly for me. Once I returned to the new home following the wedding, without Elimelek to direct the running of the flocks and fields, Mahlon needed my help much more than he expected or liked. I found solace in knowing my son needed me. Even more solace came because I was kept too busy during the day to wallow in worry that threatened to consume me during the night when I was alone with my thoughts. Yet, alone at night, I often remained unable to sleep, wondering about Kilion, King Eglon, my people in Ephrathah, and everything else.

Mateo, for his part, did indeed keep communication flowing between King Eglon and Mahlon. Mahlon often included me in the messages back and forth simply to make sure he was not saying or doing the wrong thing.

Along with the communication from the king, occasional word came from Kilion. My primary worries seemed centered on my youngest son being away from me and totally immersed in the culture of the Moabites, who had no love for our God. Every message from my youngest son was bittersweet. His messages sounded forced, and I worried all the more despite Mateo's assurances that Kilion was safe, well, and finding life among the king's court inviting.

Then there was living with my oldest son and the two Moabites among us: his young bride and Mateo, the ever-watchful emissary. I found it easy to ignore or avoid Mateo. He was nothing to me, and I made it known that I did not care to have him around me unless Mahlon needed him to be there. The old man seemed to share my aversion for he kept his distance, choosing to spend his days following in Mahlon's shadow for reasons I could not fathom.

Ruth, on the other hand, was entirely different. At first, I found it hard to trust the young woman, but as the days turned into weeks, and the weeks into months, Ruth showed herself to be a willing participant in the life of a landowner. I often found Ruth up ahead of all the rest of the household. She had to be taught a great deal, but she was a quick learner and often took the initiative to get even the most mundane chores done without being asked.

After so many months of living in close quarters with the young woman, I found myself admiring and even liking Ruth. I found Ruth to be like I had been at her age. In doing so, I found the younger woman to be a better woman than I was for she never complained. She asked a lot of questions, sometimes uncomfortable questions. Sometimes she was too forward, but she was quick, intelligent, and showed genuine interest. She truly seemed to care for Mahlon, and I reflected it had taken me much longer to grow accustomed to and fond of Elimelek. Our marriage had also been an arranged one. I thanked God for the little miracle that was Ruth, a bright spot in an otherwise bitter life for me.

During my morning prayer, rife with conflicting feelings and reflections on all that had transpired with our family since arriving in Moab, I was startled when Ruth burst into my room. "Naomi! Ima! Mateo has asked to speak with you. He says it's urgent."

I blinked and grimaced to myself. *Lord, that man. Please, Lord, remove that man from our home. Draw him back to his own people.*

I blinked again and rose to my feet before turning to Ruth, who stood in the doorway. She stood in the same kind of wool halug and robes that I wore; long gone were the wispy lengths of light and silky fabrics she had been accustomed to in the palace. Even the rough woven robes did not diminish Ruth's subtle beauty. I also noted that Ruth had not yet taken the time to braid her hair as she was used to doing to keep it out of her work, and that gave me reason to move faster.

What can that man want that is so urgent, I wondered.

I followed Ruth to the main room of the house where Mateo and Mahlon sat on woven mats. The men were silent when we entered. Ruth stood to the side of the door, but Mateo motioned for me to have a seat. I scowled at the man then looked to Mahlon who nodded and also motioned for me to have a seat.

"Kilion..." I started as it occurred to me: something must have happened to my precious son.

Mateo interrupted, "No. Your son is just fine. I need to talk to you about very specific business."

I glanced at Mahlon and noted the look of indignation on his face. I took a seat next to Mahlon and stared hard at Mateo. "Out with it then. What is so important that my prayers had to be interrupted?"

Mateo frowned. He knew how important my prayer time was to me, so he must have been on an errand from the king. He leaned toward me. "I have asked your son, and he insists he knows nothing, so I must ask you as well. How well do you know the leaders among your people in Ephrathah and beyond?"

I raised an eyebrow at the question. "I don't," I stated simply.

Mateo smirked at me. He clearly thought I was hiding something. "Come now, Naomi. We know your husband was a wealthy man in Ephrathah. Surely he was counted among the leaders of your hometown?"

I shook my head. "Had he been a leader among my people, we would never have left for his responsibility would have been to his people even above us, his family."

Mateo pressed his lips together before he replied, "That may be, but even so, as a wealthy man he would have moved in the very circles as the leaders of your town, no?"

"No," I stated flatly. "What is this all about?"

Mateo stared at me; I stared back without looking away. He knew I had no reason to lie. I made it no secret that I wanted nothing more than to return to Ephrathah before my sons were married. Now I had no desire to return to a home where they would be outcasts because of their marriages. He also knew I wasn't likely to lie and jeopardize the blessing from Eglon. Finally, he nodded. He accepted my answer, but he did not answer my question. Instead, he rose to his feet and shook out his robes.

He started to leave when Mahlon stood up suddenly and gripped the older man's arm. "Wait. My mother asked you a question, and I believe you owe us both an answer."

Mateo tried to break Mahlon's grip, but found that the young man was much stronger than he looked. Realizing he must give us some sort of answer, Mateo responded, "I got a message from King Eglon. Your people are due to send tribute as the king demanded.

There has been a lengthy delay, and my king merely wants to know who to..."

Mahlon finished, "Who to kill to get things rolling again?"

Mateo did not deny the accusation. He met Mahlon's glare with one of his own.

"Young Mahlon, you would be wise to remember you are a guest among my people with a blessing from my king. Your people fell to my people, and so my king, who is now your king, expects and demands his tribute as was promised."

Mahlon's face turned red, and he let go of Mateo's arm. "I remember everything, Mateo."

Still seated on the mat, I looked at Mateo with sudden curiosity. How much power did Mateo have over our current success among the Moabite people? How much of his observation drove the king's own hand for or against someone? I shuddered to think of what might happen if Mateo found reason to tell the king unseemly things about Mahlon.

I rose quickly and moved to diffuse the situation. Ignoring Mateo, I turned my attention entirely to Mahlon. "Son, come. I have something I want to show you."

I noted Ruth nodding and stepping to aid me in drawing Mahlon away from Mateo.

Mahlon stared darkly at the older man for a few seconds and then turned his attention first to me then to Ruth. The darkness in his eyes disappeared, and he allowed us to lead him from the room and out to a field where I suddenly found interest in the rate the barley was growing.

ELEVEN

I knelt in prayer as I looked down the hill where just a year before we had first made camp. Below me was another camp now though it was much larger and quite different from what ours had been. It was an army of Moabites ready to march against my people. King Eglon was still waiting on tribute, but it appeared one of the Judean judges or maybe many of the judges had kept the king waiting. Or maybe they had withheld the tribute as an act of defiance. Either way, King Eglon's response was to build his army and march on my people to take his tribute by force.

Watching and praying silently, I noted the variety of men gathered below me. There were men who appeared to be Mateo's age, white-haired men stooped with age. There were the middle-aged men, men closer to Elimelek's age were he still alive. Those men made up the bulk of the force. They laughed loudly, shouting cries of war and violence. Promises of what they intended to do to their enemies washed up the hill on the wind and turned my blood to ice. Then there were the younger men and the boys. I was thankful there were not as many though the number of boys that from a distance didn't even appear to have any facial hair yet made me weep inside. The youngest of them cowered at every yell and scream. They had not yet seen violence; they certainly had not acted in violence.

Oh, Lord, be with those children. Lord, let them return to their mothers. Lord, please spare the youth.

The head of the camp, a brutal-looking man, had requested food and water from Mahlon. Unable to refuse the request, Mahlon himself took a cartload of both to the encampment. Young men, middle-aged men, and even old men gathered around the cart for food and water to add to their supplies. Mateo had given Mahlon a warning that the army would pass by, which enabled Mahlon to have the cart loaded with what supplies he felt we could spare. Mateo had also informed Mahlon that for now the army was made only of men who volunteered to serve their king. As I stared at the young men below me, I wondered how many families volunteered their own young men to gain favor with the king. I recalled Mateo's warning that should the advance into Judah fail to bring the king his desired results, he would send a larger army, one that would require more men to the point of enlisting them against their will.

I recalled the demand Mateo made because he felt Mahlon should volunteer, that it was his duty as a son of the king to do so. I was relieved when my son addressed that matter bluntly and directly by telling Mateo that he would heed the call when, and only when, the king himself asked him to do so. He expressed he was certain the king would not want his eldest daughter left unprotected so far from Kir-Moab. Mateo had no argument for that, so he grudgingly let the subject close. I was convinced it would not be the end of the matter for Mateo regarding Mahlon.

After I witnessed that conversation between Mateo and Mahlon, I wondered about Kilion. Was he impressed upon to volunteer? Would the king imply it was Kilion's duty? What if Kilion was among the men below? Would my youngest volunteer to fight for a man like Eglon? To fight against our own people?

At the thoughts, I forced my eyes shut to block out the distraction of the army below me, and I lost myself in desperate prayer for the safety of my youngest son, no matter where he might be. I remained at the top of the slope, deep in prayer and stillness, until I heard the rumble of the wheels. Opening my eyes, I watched as Mahlon began his journey back up the slope. I watched him for several minutes, noting his slumped shoulders and the way he stared at the ground. Finally, I returned my gaze to the camp where they were already preparing to leave. I sighed in relief but again wondered about Kilion.

Lord, no matter where he is, please keep him safe. Lord, please be with all these men. Please let justice prevail. If they fall in battle, Lord, let their death be swift. Lord, please be with my people, with your people. Please help them overcome and find favor in Your sight.

Soft steps approached from behind me, and I turned to see who it might be.

Ruth caught my eye and sat on the ground next to me, her gaze moving to the men working below us.

"So many would willingly throw their lives away."

I raised my eyebrows at the younger woman's comment, but I replied, "So many would argue that a life given in service to your father, the king, is a gift and a show of loyal devotion."

Ruth looked at me, "My father.... Yes. I imagine you're right, but we both know some of those men won't come home. They have to know that they could be sacrificing everything. Still they go to a far-off place to take tribute from people who hate us."

She paused and took a deep breath, continuing on with anger and frustration raising her voice, "They go off to that place, far from the people who love them to will-ingly surround themselves by people who hate them. I am not sure how my father justifies this. He knows Judah is still amid the long famine. What little those people have, they need to survive. Demanding tribute off the backs of the starving. What does it achieve?"

Ruth stopped abruptly, and I realized the younger woman had let her tongue get the best of her. Had she said that anywhere near Mateo, and her words reached her father's ears.... The thought was scary indeed.

I reached over and took Ruth's hand. "Ruth, I have made no secret that my people are a separate people and that our Lord has told us to remain separate. However, our Lord has never told us to hate the people we are to be separate from. Though you are right, my people will fight fiercely to keep what God has given them."

Ruth took a deep breath and visibly relaxed. She squeezed my hand gently. "I just don't understand. In time of war, in time of violence, there is only love and hate, nothing in between. There is the idea of love we have for something that drives us to protect what we love, or there is hate for the thing that we think threatens the thing we love."

I nodded. The young woman's words rang true, and we both knew it. In silence, we continued to watch the army below until the camp was taken down and the army slowly marched away. How would war affect us?

TWELVE

Rudely wakened in early morning hours by soldiers banging on the door, I opened the door to our home and was roughly pushed aside as Mateo barreled in, looking exhausted and unkempt. He had been called away a few months earlier to assist Bahio and King Eglon, but when he left, he had given Mahlon no answer regarding his return. Yet there he stood, staring around him with clear disgust.

Mahlon broke the tension between Mateo and me when he entered the room, his eyes wide, his jaw set. "What is the meaning of this, Mateo?"

He glared at Mahlon. "As if you didn't know..."

Ruth entered and stood by Mahlon's side. "Mateo, please. You've woken us in the middle of the night. Welcome back, but what is all this commotion about?"

Mateo forced his expression to one of deference to his princess, and he bowed to her. "My apologies. I fear I have sad tidings."

Ruth leaned on Mahlon, fatigue plain on her face. He wrapped an arm around her shoulders, while I stood motionless with my hand still on the latch to the door.

Mateo licked his lips, suddenly apprehensive. "Your Grace, your father, the king... he was killed."

Ruth's eyes grew round, and her face pale, but she continued to lean on Mahlon. "Killed?" she asked. "How? I was told he would not be leading the army himself. He was staying behind..."

Mateo shook his head. Just as he was about to speak, he was pushed aside and I found myself staring at Kilion and Orpah behind him, both dirty and weary looking.

"What is going on here?" demanded Kilion as he rushed into the room and began dusting his clothes off. "Mateo, you were supposed to announce us and then come get us!"

Mateo bowed his head but did not reply while I moved away from the door and approached my son, whom I had not seen in over a year.

"My son..." I began, but Orpah interrupted, "Kil, this is not suitable for us. We should move on..."

Kilion whirled toward Orpah, his eyes flashing. "Where would you have us go? We can't return to the very place your father was murdered. You saw what was happening. Bahio and your brother, the rightful king, were killed after word reached the people of your father's death. They are in full revolt! We can't go on to the home of your mother, because we have known for months now that your uncle has no intention of recognizing Ruth, you, or any of your sisters as heirs to the throne."

Orpah flushed and glanced at Ruth, who simply stared back at her half-sister.

"Father..." began Ruth, and Orpah nodded silently. The sisters rushed to each other and sank to a bench in a tearful embrace while Mateo resumed his hateful glare at Mahlon and then at Kilion. "Your people did this."

Mahlon raised his hands to quiet the older man, glancing at the weeping women as he did so. Mateo quickly shut his mouth and allowed Mahlon to lead him out of the house and into the brightening dawn.

Once outside with Kilion standing to one side and me on the other, Mahlon motioned for Mateo to explain himself. "A judge from your people has been coming to Eglon as an emissary with talks of peace."

Mahlon shrugged his shoulders and looked to Kilion. "So? What does that have to do with us?"

Kilion frowned in Mateo's direction. "Apparently this old fool thinks we all know each other, so we must all be conspiring with each other."

"Wait, I'm confused. We know who? One of the judges? What happened?"

"Kilion spoke for the man." Mateo stated.

Mahlon looked at his brother.

"I spoke for him; I don't deny it. The man I spoke for was one of our people. I thought because he was one of our judges that he could be trusted. I never imagined..."

Mateo interrupted, "You say that, yet you were seen talking to him on multiple occasions in secret."

Kilion rolled his eyes. "It must not have been that secret if I was seen talking to him so many times."

Mateo grunted, but continued, "This emissary, this judge you call Ehud, Kilion spoke for and gained our king's trust. Then when the king least expected it – he had in fact sent this emissary back to your people with a plan for peace..."

Kilion coughed. "A plan for peace, you say. It was a plan to enslave our young men. To make them soldiers in your army. It was a plan to further increase the demands for tribute so your people could try to conquer more people."

Mateo did not deny Kilion's accusation but instead wore a smug smile. "Regardless, your man was supposed to be on his way back to your people. Instead, he snuck back into the palace and ran our king through, killing him."

Mahlon ran a hand over his face and stared at Kilion and Mateo. Mahlon had no love for Mateo, and he was not exactly sure where his own brother stood on the matter. He made it sound like he was disgusted by the king's methods, but he also lived like a prince with

Orpah and her people. He met Kilion's eyes, and they stared at each other for several long minutes, each one trying to read the other.

Finally, Mahlon turned his gaze to me. "Mother, can Kilion and Orpah have your room? Do you mind?"

I nodded in agreement. I didn't care what brought my son back or what I had to give up to keep him under my roof. I'd sleep with the sheep if it meant my boys were back with me.

Kilion moved to stand in front of me. He seemed taller to me after a year. He was clean shaven. His hair was trimmed short as was the style for the Moabites. In his clear eyes, I saw both a stranger and my son. I stretched my arms out to embrace him, but he pushed my arms down to my side and gave me a peck on my forehead.

"Thank you, Mother." He turned to Mahlon, "I better ready the room. Orpah has high standards. It has to be just right, or she will insist we go back. It's just not safe."

Mahlon nodded and watched Kilion move into the house. Through the open door, we could hear Ruth and Orpah talking and crying. Mateo shuffled his feet. "Ruth and Orpah do not belong here. By right, Ruth should be queen..."

Mahlon spun on his heel and glared at Mateo. "Ruth wants none of that, and you will not try to persuade her otherwise."

Mateo glared back at Mahlon. "You forget yourself. She is the queen now. It is her choice and her choice alone."

I spoke up, "But her uncle..."

Mateo stepped back and sighed. "Her uncle. Yes. He will have to be dealt with, but once he is, Ruth will be made queen."

Mahlon rolled his eyes and turned toward the house without another word. I watched him go and noted the sudden slouch in his posture. Mahlon did indeed love Ruth. They were a good match, but was he right about Ruth? Faced with being queen, would she still choose the simple life she led beside Mahlon? Mateo clearly didn't think so.

I turned to Mateo. "Is her uncle seeking the throne for himself?"

Mateo nodded.

"So Ruth and Orpah are in danger?"

He nodded again.

"But if Ruth abdicates?"

Mateo shook his head. "No. She cannot..."

"But if she did?"

Mateo looked off into the distance. "If she did, she would be put into exile. Orpah too. They would lose all their rights and privileges as heirs to the king and as royal lineage for our people. They would have nothing. Be nothing. Just commoners."

I nodded. "I see. So you want to stop fighting with my people and begin fighting your own so that Ruth can take the throne?"

Mateo grimaced. "You know nothing, woman. I want to fight for my queen to allow her to keep what is already hers."

"But you would be fighting and killing your own people."

"The king's brother, her uncle, already is. In his search for her, he is killing everything that gets in his way. Bahio included."

"It must stop, Mateo," interrupted Ruth.

Both Mateo and I jumped at Ruth's voice. She stepped out of the darkness and closer to the fire. Her face was streaked with tears, and her eyes were red. Her face was puffy and swollen from crying over her father.

"I expect you to help end this," she responded in a low voice.

Mateo nodded eagerly. "We must get you back to the palace immediately."

"No. My place is here. You will go to find my uncle and tell him I accept exile. I will not leave my husband, and I will not take the throne. I cannot; I do not have the heart for it."

Mateo's eyes grew round and anger lit a fire in them. "What have these people done to you? They have ruined you. Brainwashed you. Driven you mad!"

"If it is madness to want an end to bloodshed, so be it. If it is madness to find joy in simplicity, so be it. I was never interested in following in my father's footsteps. So you get whatever you need to make this official with my uncle, and let's get it done."

Mateo grumbled, "He will probably still want your head. Both your heads. And the heads of these interlopers too."

Ruth frowned at the old man. "You will do what you do best, Mateo. You will see my wishes carried out, and you will work out a way for us to keep our heads."

Mateo nodded and shrugged. "I will finally be free of you."

His comment, directed at me, earned him a nearly jubilant smile from me and a scowl from Ruth. He looked back at Ruth. "I will see your wishes are carried out, but once it's done, you will no longer have me to serve you."

Ruth nodded. "I expect my uncle will want you at his side once he is king."

Mateo nodded mutely.

Ruth gripped her hands tightly in front of her. She seemed to suddenly age and mature in front of me while also looking so young and vulnerable. I prayed silently for the Lord to bless Ruth's decision to take herself and her sister into exile.

THIRTEEN

M onths passed slowly, turning into long years. The Moabites continued to fight against the Hebrews as well as other surrounding peoples. I prayed without ceasing that the Lord would protect my family. Once Ruth had sent Mateo away, we worried and waited for weeks afterward, expecting Mateo to return to make her abdication official. But he never returned.

Word spread throughout the land that King Eglon's brother was a more cruel and suspicious man than Eglon had been to the point that he put Eglon's advisors, generals, and their entire families to death. Ruth and Orpah lived in fear that soldiers would track them down to arrest them and put them to death as well, but as those first weeks passed and turned into months, their fears gradually diminished.

Meanwhile, battles and skirmishes waged on and off in the distance. Sometimes soldiers would stop by our land demanding a share of our food, water, and goods, but beyond rough handling and often intimidating threats that they never followed up on, they never tarried longer than a day or two.

The fields that Mahlon and Kilion tended were well-groomed and abundantly fruitful. With Ruth and Orpah to help, we earned the trust and respect of the local tribal people, and over time, the fields became as much the local people's as they were Mahlon's.

I swelled with pride at how thoughtful he was concerning the people that lived all around us. He was often gone for days at a time, helping people around the countryside and sharing whatever we could afford to share. Ruth also shared in Mahlon's willingness to help, often traveling with him when we knew he would be gone for more than a day.

Kilion and Orpah, however, remained close to home. With their sudden reduction in social and financial status, they struggled to find meaning and to define their relationship with each other and with our family. Kilion threw himself into the business of the land and livestock. He worked himself every day to exhaustion, barely able to stand and interact once he retired from the fields for the day. He withdrew into himself, avoiding everyone except Mahlon.

Orpah, no longer the center of Kilion's world or the center of attention, became even more demanding and impatient. Worse, she often found that the only person to talk to was me, but she found me to be too blunt and too demanding. Still, as her fears of being discovered faded, so too did her bitterness and anger. She did not blame Ruth for turning Mateo away. Nor could she blame Kilion or me for her reduced circumstances. Slowly, I guess she decided to make the best of things, and she gradually warmed up to me. The more Kilion withdrew from her, the more she turned to me. I sensed she longed for love and approval after finding none in her husband.

Through all this, I fought the growing seed of bitterness that had taken root when we left Ephrathah so many years before. I saw the land around us being blessed, but it was not my home. I continued to beg and plead with the Lord to work in leading my sons back to Ephrathah. Over the years, I had brought returning to Ephrathah up to Mahlon. He simply cast a warning glance at me, and he would dismiss the idea immediately. As I finally realized that my sons would never return home on their own, I prayed for distraction to keep my mind from my pain and bitterness. I prayed the Lord would give me grandchildren.

Ruth screamed out as labor pains wracked her body. Seated at Ruth's feet, I rubbed her legs and feet and sang a song I remembered my mother singing when my sons were born. Orpah sat at Ruth's head and wiped her brow.

"This is the one, Ru. I can feel it."

Ruth, tears streaming down her face, tried to smile at her sister. "I don't think so, Orpah. Something is wrong."

My face screwed up in concern at Ruth's words. Pushing Ruth's legs apart, I pressed a hand inward to feel for the baby. Ruth appeared to be giving birth way too early again, but the time leading up to her sudden labor pains had been uneventful. She had not even experienced morning sickness. As I felt for the baby, my hand touched the crown of its head. Finding it in the correct position, I sighed with relief.

"Ruth, my girl, you push those negative thoughts away. The head is right and nearly ready for you to push. You both start saying those prayers as I taught you. Pray the Lord grants us a strong young boy for Mahlon."

Orpah leaned over her sister and hugged her tight. "It will be all right, Ru. You'll see."

Ruth nodded her head and started reciting prayers I had taught her. In the back of my mind, I prayed my own prayer and begged the Lord to help Ruth give Mahlon an heir finally.

I continued to keep one hand on the baby's head while I reached into the cervix with my other hand and felt that Ruth was still not dilated enough. "Don't push yet, my girl. Not yet. Your body needs a little more time."

I looked at Orpah. "I need you to get my herbs and hot water. Quickly now."

Orpah kissed Ruth on the forehead. "I'll be right back. Don't have this baby without me."

Ruth managed a weak smile at her sister, and I grimaced as she arched her back and tried rolling from one side to the other. Watching her writhe in pain, I knew what she was feeling. I recalled all too well, even at my age, the power of labor pains as they ripped through our feminine bodies, through our abdomens and lower backs.

"I have to push!" she cried out at me.

I withdrew the hand that was investigating the cervix and gently squeezed Ruth's leg. "No, child. Do not push. The child won't fit through just yet. Breathe deeply and work to calm yourself. Orpah is bringing my herbs. I have something you can drink that might help. Just don't push."

Ruth threw her head back and sobbed in pain and frustration.

Finally, Orpah rushed back in and sat beside me as I wiped my hands on a clean cloth before I rummaged through my bag of herbs. I found a small satchel of dried leaves and ground a pinch into the hot water. "Here. Give this to her. Make sure she drinks it all."

Orpah took the herbal tea and moved to Ruth's side. She helped Ruth lift her head and sip the hot fluid. Once it was all gone, Orpah set the cup on the floor, and she held Ruth's hands.

"Is the pain very bad?" she asked.

Ruth stared into her sister's eyes. We all knew Orpah would never have children of her own. Long before marrying Kilion, Orpah had been overly flirtatious and welcoming to men. After many flirtations led to pregnancies, and those pregnancies led to abortions either by the king's doctors or by backstreet midwives with strange concoctions, Orpah had been warned over and over that she wasn't likely to get pregnant again. True enough, after marrying Kilion and them being together for nearly ten years, she had not gotten pregnant even once. Meanwhile, Ruth got pregnant time after time, but had yet to deliver a healthy baby.

We wondered at the strange hand at work. Surely God would not allow Ruth to get pregnant over and over just to take the child away during birth every single time. This was now Ruth's sixth pregnancy.

She smiled bravely at Orpah. "No, the pain is not so bad. Not as bad as last time," she lied, hoping we wouldn't be able to tell.

Orpah smiled. "Good. That's a good sign."

Both women looked at me. I had been so blessed by these two loving sisters. So much time had passed, and the three of us had grown fond of each other. We had grown to rely on each other. Now I could tell Ruth was lying and that Orpah knew it just as I did, but I saw love in the lies. I saw love and hope. I smiled at the younger women and nodded.

"Let's see if that tea is helping," I said.

I reinserted my hand into Ruth's cervix and, finding the baby's head, I compared it to the opening. I worked to keep the frown off my face. The baby had stopped struggling against the opening, and the opening had not gotten any larger at all as far as I could tell.

Lord, I pled inwardly, *not this one too. Please, Lord. Please, grant us this little blessing.*

Ruth's body involuntarily shifted as the labor pains hit again. Nearly lifting off the floor in pain, Ruth cried out and could hold back no longer. She followed her instincts and pushed hard, willing the baby out of her body. All her thoughts and rationale flew away as pain enveloped her and drove her to do what her body demanded be done.

After what felt like an eternity, Ruth collapsed onto the blankets, her face red and sweaty. Tears streamed down her face, and she sobbed openly. She didn't need me to confirm what she already knew.

The baby had been stillborn.

FOURTEEN

I heard Mahlon and Kilion talking in low voices outside the house. I got up and dressed for the day but paused when I heard a third voice and then two others. Mahlon asked someone to calm down while Kilion's voice rose in anger. I rushed to the window and peered into the dim morning light.

Three men stood before my sons with weapons in their hands. One man appeared to be a soldier, but the other two were men I recognized from nearby. I stood still, my hands wringing the edge of my robe as I listened to Mahlon try to diffuse the situation. I realized it didn't matter what Mahlon said, Kilion was clearly ready for a fight. His own weapon was drawn from his belt and held ready before him. I felt the color drain from my face as the men's voices grew even louder.

"Ima, what is it?"

I jumped at Ruth's whispered voice right behind me.

I whispered back to her, "I'm not sure. Please go wake Orpah. We need to be ready."

Ruth peered over my shoulder and saw the men squaring off in the yard. "Ready? For what?"

My stomach lurch as dread set in. I looked into Ruth's eyes. "Ready to run."

Ruth stepped back and stared at me for a moment, not comprehending what I meant, but then she looked back out the window and saw Mahlon raise his hands in a show of submission. She watched with me as one of the armed men stepped toward Mahlon instead of backing down. In an instant, Ruth rushed from the room in search of Orpah, while I remained at the window and prayed for the Lord's intervention for our family's safety.

In slow motion, my prayers shattered as Kilion rushed toward the soldier who had confronted Mahlon and slashed at him. Instantly, one of the other men stepped to block Kilion's rush and stabbed forward, catching Kilion in his gut and dropping him to the ground. Mahlon stood frozen for a moment while the three men stepped over Kilion and moved closer to him.

I watched in terror as the men circled Mahlon and taunted him with the promise of torture and abuse for him and for the rest of us. They promised Mahlon a slow death. But first, they promised, he would watch them rape and torture any women in the house and then torture and kill any other men around as well.

Mahlon turned in a slow circle, watching the men. He had not drawn his own knife. Maybe he still hoped to talk the men down, but as he turned, he caught sight of his brother lying unmoving in a growing pool of blood, then of me staring silently out the window. At that moment, I saw hope leave his eyes, and I saw him lash out in blind fury.

In a flash of motion, he pulled his knife out and lunged at one of the men. He dealt that man a killing blow with a wild slash at the man's neck, but before he could turn to defend himself from the other two, he was stabbed in his back and shoulder. He sank to the ground, but the men stepped back from him, unwilling to kill him. I realized they were intent on keeping their promise to him. Even in the house, I heard the men taunting him, but beyond that, I heard the thumping of my heart.

My eldest gritted his teeth as he pushed himself to his feet. He glanced at the window where I was watching. I met his gaze, hoping I could convey to him I would do whatever I could to keep Ruth and Orpah safe. I knew even as my heart shattered, my son was going to make sure those men would never reach us. He was prepared to die for us.

One man watched Mahlon rise from the ground, and he stepped forward to push Mahlon back down, but Mahlon grabbed the man's leg and yanked it as hard as he could. In his weakened state, he succeeded in making the man fall, but he fell with him. He took advantage of the fall as he brought his knife to bear on the man so that as he fell with the man, the weight of the fall pushed the blade deep into the man's chest.

After the impact, he lost his breath, but he rolled to his back and moved his head to look for the third attacker. The man had already closed the gap and stood over Mahlon with a wicked sneer on his face. He opened his mouth and started to speak but was cut short as I slammed a shovel down on his head with such force that the man fell dead to the ground.

Mahlon stared at me with the shovel in my hands. As he blacked out, I desperately called his name. My cries were joined by a shriek of dismay from Ruth as she ran to him from the house.

FIFTEEN

The rule of the land dictated that widows be given a week's time to mourn before decisions be made regarding ownership of their husband's belongings. As we grieved for Mahlon and Kilion, we also noted the number of people from our community who suddenly showed an interest in us. One after another, men and women from the area came to offer us their condolences, but each one failed to hide their curiosity about who would claim the house and the land that we had worked to make prosperous.

The well-kept land with its fields, our small herds, and our home was of great value, but because I was a widow and a foreigner, the Moabites would never buy it from me. I would be forced to give it away and hope that whoever took it would keep me on as a servant. With regret and sadness, I knew that Ruth and Orpah would have to rely on that charity as well until they could remarry. For that entire week, I struggled over what to do, who to give the land to, but I could come to no good resolution.

Finally, late in the middle of the seventh night, I woke to a thought. It was an ugly thought, and I felt ungrateful for having it, but I also felt it was the perfect solution. I did not stop to ponder the repercussions, but I woke Ruth and Orpah with grim determination, telling them to pack our belongings onto a couple of pack mules. I ignored their questions until after they were packed and dressed for traveling, my sense of urgency driving the younger women to hurry even though they did not know what the urgency was for.

"Ima, what are we doing? The sun isn't even up yet." Orpah asked around a wide yawn.

I reached out and took Orpah's hand then reached for Ruth's hand as well. "It's time for us to leave this wretched place."

Ruth squeezed my hand gently, her own eyes puffy and red with the grief she still felt over Mahlon's tragic death. "Leave? But to where?"

I drew the younger women in close and whispered to them, "Go wake the servants. Have them gather whatever they want. Tell them they are free. Tell them to leave the house at once."

Ruth and Orpah looked at each other in confusion, but the manner in which I spoke left no room for argument. They hurried through the house, waking everyone. By sunrise, despite the confusion and anger, only the three of us remained.

While the young women watched the last of the servants disappear out of sight, I grabbed one of the oil lanterns and dumped the oil on the floor of the room where I had tried so desperately to save Elimelek. I called Ruth and Orpah to come into the house, instructing them to do the same. Now fully alarmed, Ruth and Orpah did as they were asked, but they were both clearly scared. The obvious decision that I had made loomed over them. After several long minutes, they met me at the door to the house.

"Ima, are you going to destroy it all?" Ruth asked with sad dread touching her voice.

"This is crazy," added Orpah. "We'll have nothing left. We'll be completely destitute."

I sighed heavily, the bitterness in my voice cold as ice. "We already have nothing. We lost it all when we lost our men. I will not allow the people who killed our men, who lusted over the things we worked so hard for. They will not have it. They will not have us."

Without another word, I took a burning log from the cooking fire and carefully laid it in a stream of oil. I watched in silence as the oil lit and spread through one room and then another. After I was content that the fire could not be put out, I turned to Ruth and Orpah, who stood staring at me in astonishment. I frowned, knowing they thought I had lost my mind, but I was never more certain about anything in my life.

Striding past my daughters, I grabbed one mule by its lead and started walking away from the house. Ruth said something to Orpah and then I heard them both follow. I glanced over my shoulder to see the young women leading the second mule after me.

Behind us, flames from the burning house started to reach out of the windows and touch the wood of the roof. It would not be long before it was completely engulfed, and I smiled. Considering how the Lord had turned his back on my family, I was certain this was the only justice I would ever know for the horror the Moabites had inflicted on my family. It was not much, but it was something. Yet as I walked away, the sun climbing higher into the sky, I also felt shame and sadness.

Lord, forgive me. Please tell me that this pain will go away. Please show me where to go now. What do I do now?

I stared into the light of the morning sun but heard and felt nothing but pain, sadness, and that ever-growing seed of bitterness. At the back of my mind, a nagging thought that had haunted me now for so long grew louder.

God was not listening.

God had forsaken me and my family long ago. Maybe He would never hear me again. Now after exacting my own kind of revenge, could I expect any different? If He never answered me again, it would be my own fault. So lost in my dismay, I moved on down the road toward the Dead Sea, barely aware of the two young women who wandered behind me with the weight of their own fears, doubts, and grief heavy on their shoulders.

SIXTEEN

"Ru, where do you think she's leading us?" Orpah whispered, not realizing I could hear her even from where I lay.

Ruth and Orpah shared a blanket next to the small fire I had built after realizing we couldn't go on another step without food and rest. Ruth looked over her sister's head and glanced in my direction. I don't think she could see that I was still awake. Through slit eyes, I watched her stare in my direction before she turned her attention back to her sister.

"I don't know where she will lead us. I don't think she knows. Not yet. But I think she will hear from Yahweh even if she doesn't realize He's speaking. Mother has lost everything, and I fear she has lost her faith as well."

Orpah looked over her shoulder at Ruth, her whisper loud and harsh, "Do you think her god cares about her? About us? I see her pray day after day. She prays the prayers her mother taught her, and she prays her own prayers, but all I see is each prayer left unanswered."

Ruth stopped combing Orpah's hair. What was going through the young woman's mind? Both of them had just witnessed their husbands murdered by their own people. Watching their people kill Elimelek had been horrifying, but I was not shocked our enemy would do something like that. However, after ten years of watching their husbands work so hard to become trusted among the Moabites, it had to hurt even more to be betrayed in such a devastating way.

Orpah continued, "If her god is real, he's most cruel, Ru. Most cruel. Especially to Naomi. Even to you. What kind of god would take away a husband or a child? And so brutally every time?"

I felt myself cringe inwardly as I agreed with Orpah. My God, Yahweh, had proven over and over to be brutal to me, to mine.

Ruth kneeled back to rest on her heels. She sat silently for a while, but I waited to hear her response. Was she as angry at God as I was?

"I don't know. I know Naomi asks those same questions. Yet despite all this hardship and pain, she still knows Him to be real. I don't know how to explain it. I don't know that she knows how to explain it. However, for her to still know Him, for her to still pray, that means that He is as real to her as you and I are. He is tangible."

Orpah huffed in exasperation, "I will never understand it."

And again, I agreed with both young women. Ruth was right. Despite it all, I knew my God to still be present. The question that burned inside me had nothing to do with Him being real or not but had everything to do with Him forsaking my family.

Ruth began combing Orpah's hair again then wove strands together in a series of braids that she tied together with a piece of leather cord. When she finished, she tapped Orpah on the shoulder. The two lay side by side on the wide blanket, and I prayed they drew comfort from each other.

After listening to them speak, I tossed and turned. I desperately wanted to get lost in sleep, my heart heavy with grief and my mind at war with itself. I just wanted to close my eyes and let it all end. I thought back to the events of the day.

As soon as we had lost sight of the house that morning, I regretted burning it. I regretted the shame and guilt I felt over giving up and putting us at risk simply to grasp at some desperate form of justice. The entire time we had been trekking, I had fought the urge to run back to see if we could salvage the home, but I knew it was no use. We couldn't go back, and we had nowhere to go forward to.

After I was certain Orpah and Ruth had fallen asleep, I quietly moved to a kneeling position. With the fire at my back, I stared up into the night sky.

"Dear Lord, where are you? Where have you gone? Why have you abandoned us? Was Elimelek's lack of faith so horrendous that you had to take not just him, but my sons as well? Lord, forgive me..." I stopped as anger and grief battled within me and the urge to scream and shout nearly overcame me. I forced myself to take several deep breaths to get my emotions under control. "Lord, we desperately need you. Please show us the path we should take. Please guide our steps. Lord, please heal our hearts. Please heal my heart. I feel like it's been broken for so long it no longer knows how to beat. Lord, please, for the sake of these young women, show us mercy."

Suddenly, the sky above me lit up as a shooting star flashed across it. I stared after it. For a split second, my heart jumped at the sight, but then doubt washed over me and I wondered if it was a sign.

Was God still listening? After all this time, did He care at all?

I bowed my head and recited the prayers of my people. One after another, I recited them all in a low whisper, my fingers rubbing at the hem of my halug as I prayed. I hoped that speaking the prayers into the night would help soothe my soul, but once I had finished all the ones I could remember, I lay down still feeling hollow and riddled with physical and emotional pain.

Feeling lost inside, I listened to the crackle of the fire while I watched wispy clouds travel across the night sky, blotting out stars here and there as they traveled. My last thought as I finally drifted off to restless sleep was that sunrise would be a new day, and with the sunrise, we would have to make some serious decisions.

SEVENTEEN

We walked wearily ahead of the pack mules, saying very little. None of us knew what to say that could make anything better. None of us had any ideas of where to go, whom to turn to in our time of need. I kept silently praying even though my heart was hard as stone. Even as the prayers flowed out of me, they felt hollow. I was praying just to pray, more to keep my sanity than to actually get an answer from God.

I knew Ruth prayed silently as well. I could sense her deep sadness, but since she had become part of our family and learned of our God, she'd embraced our teachings and then embraced our faith. I had taught her some of our prayers and songs, but Mahlon had taught her much more. In his love for Ruth, he'd discovered renewed faith. Even though he never felt led to return to Ephrathah, he rejoiced in every blessing. He displayed kindness and courage with the Moabites, and in doing so, he exhibited more of our faith and more of our God than I did. And Ruth reveled in the faith he shared with her. I hoped she could still find some semblance of peace within our faith even if I could not.

Orpah was harder for me to gauge. I knew she missed the parties and decadence she had enjoyed when her father lived. I often wondered if she wished her father had not given her to Kilion. Had she been married to someone else, her life may have looked very different for her, and she was much more likely to still be in the pampered life she had grown accustomed to if she also had the foresight to relinquish any claims to inheritance as Ruth had done. Still, she and I had grown to be friends, but she was not interested in learning our family's ways or our faith in Yahweh. The relationship we shared differed greatly from the one Ruth and I shared.

So caught up in our own thoughts, we were nearly run off the road by a merchant's caravan that rounded a sharp corner on the road we were on. We didn't even hear its approach until the merchant yelled out curses at us, making us jump and run to the side of the wide road. We must have been a horrid sight because the merchant slowed his leading cart.

"Can I be of help to you women?" he asked, no doubt thinking he might make a sale along his journey to the next Moabite settlement.

I peered up at the man but said nothing.

Ruth, however, took the initiative to get information and stepped toward the man on the wagon, her eyes boring into his.

"Could you tell us what road this is? We've been traveling hard and seem to have lost our bearings sometime last evening."

The merchant looked closely at Ruth and then at Orpah and me. I could clearly see him assessing each one of us for our value. Ruth was more plain, but she was obviously strong, while Orpah behind her was quite pretty despite the dust and dirt layered on her face and clothing. And me? I probably looked exactly as I felt: old, rundown, and completely uncaring. I watched him move his attention back to Ruth and Orpah. They were young, strong, and not ugly. They could be worth a lot of money sold as slaves. I wondered what he would do with me. I guessed he would simply leave me on the side of the road. If he wanted my daughters, there was little any of us could do to stop him.

I held my breath as he turned to his men. But then he stopped, his eyes on Ruth. I watched how he returned her stare for a few seconds. He shook his head as though trying to eradicate a thought, then he answered Ruth.

"You are on the king's highway," he responded. "If you keep heading the direction you are going, you will see the Dead Sea in the distance to the west, and then you will come to a well-trafficked crossroads. Turning toward the setting sun will take you into Judah and toward Ephrathah."

I instantly perked up and stepped forward until I could touch the front wheel of his cart. "What's the news from Ephrathah?" I asked nervously. "Are they still in the midst of that awful famine?"

The merchant laughed heartily. "Famine? By no means. I just came from there. My last wagon is full of early barley harvest from the fields around Ephrathah. It appears as devastating as the famine was, the Hebrew god has blessed his people with abundance."

I gripped the wheel tightly to keep from falling to the ground in shock at the news.

The merchant turned his attention back to Ruth. "Do you women need anything? I have many things that may interest you."

I watched Ruth, who looked at Orpah, who was staring brazenly at one of the handsome young men guarding one of the wagons. Then she looked at me. I nodded to her, knowing she was thinking clearly while I was still processing what the merchant said.

"Can we fill our skins with some of your water? I mean, we have nothing to trade, but all we need for our journey is food and water."

"Where might your journey be taking you?" asked the merchant, suddenly curious.

Ruth shrugged her shoulders dismissively. "We are going to visit family."

I sighed inwardly, thankful that she had no intention of telling the stranger the truth. But I hoped he would indeed share some food and water with us if she answered his questions.

The merchant didn't seem to pay attention to the vagueness of her answer. I stared up at him and watched his appraising expression change to one of sympathy. I wondered if he had a wife and daughters he was trying to get home to. Maybe we reminded him of them.

He turned to one of his men standing next to his cart and directed him to get us several days' provisions. Then turning back to Ruth, he said, "I have some bread, some wine, and some grapes to share with you. Will three days' worth be enough?"

Ruth shook her head emphatically, "Yes! Thank you for your graciousness!"

The merchant waved a hand at her, and we waited in silence as the food was loaded onto one of the pack mules. After it was secured, he looked suddenly embarrassed and awkward as though he realized he had given away too much and to complete strangers who had nothing to give in return.

In a sudden hurry, he bowed his head to Ruth, "I hope your journey is without incident."

Before Ruth could respond, the man flicked the reins, and his wagon moved forward briskly. In a few minutes, the small caravan left only a small cloud of settling dust with the three of us staring after them.

Ruth turned to me. Her eyes grew round with concern as she saw tears streaming down my face. "Ima, what's wrong?"

I smiled through my tears as I took Ruth's hands in my own and looked both younger women in the eyes. "Yahweh *has* been listening," I cried.

EIGHTEEN

W e sat on the ground eating and drinking from the food the merchant had given us. I couldn't help smiling at nothing as I ate my food. Ruth appeared to find my smile welcome, but Orpah was put off.

"Why are you smiling like that?" she asked me.

I looked up and held the bread before her. "Didn't you just see how the Lord provided for us? Did you not see how that merchant gave of his supplies more than we asked? Have you ever heard of a merchant just giving something away and getting nothing in return?"

Orpah frowned. "True, our meeting with the man was unusual, but maybe he just took pity on us. I cannot imagine that your god had anything to do with the man giving us a free meal."

I shrugged. "Maybe, but with this, his generosity, also came news of Judah, of Ephrathah. My dear daughters, it is time for me to return to my home."

I watched Orpah and Ruth exchange surprised glances with each other. Each had to be thinking different things. It would be a long journey for three women traveling alone on foot. The prospect was not something any of us looked forward to, but I know I must have been glowing with excitement.

I stared at both of the younger women for several minutes, women I loved as though they had been born from me. Then I took a deep breath.

"Ruth, Orpah, my daughters, my time has come to return to my home. The time has come for you both to return to the homes of your mothers, wherever they may be. If you hurry, you can catch that merchant's caravan before nightfall. I pray the Lord will be kind to you both as you were kind to my sons and then to me. I hope and pray that you will find peace and security as wives for new husbands."

Without waiting for a response from either of them, I rose to my feet. I picked up my bag and tied it to the back of one mule. Then turning to the women who now stood behind me, I took each one in my arms and kissed them on their cheeks, saying a prayer over them. Ruth and Orpah stood there mutely as though they could not fully fathom what I was suggesting, but then the realization of what I had said hit them both.

Weeping, Orpah and Ruth clung to me in immediate emotional protest.

Orpah sobbed, "No! We will go with you. We can't let you travel alone all that way."

Ruth nodded in agreement.

I shook my head as I reached out to both and touched their faces gently. "Why would you come with me? I have no sons for you to marry. I am too old to remarry at any rate. If there were even a remote chance I found a man who would take me as his wife this very day, and I conceived a son immediately, would you wait so long to remarry? *Could* you wait that long to remarry? Oh, my dear daughters, it hurts that God raised his hand against me, for your sakes, because now you are widows like me. But there is hope for you. You both are young and vibrant and will make fine wives. I beg of you to leave me on my way and seek your mothers' homes that they can help you begin again."

Orpah and Ruth wrapped their arms around me and hugged me tightly. They each nodded and kissed me then turned to pack their bags onto the remaining mule. Orpah secured hers, and I watched Ruth lift hers to the mule, but then she paused. She glanced back at me, where I was waiting for the half-sisters to leave before I turned to begin my journey. I watched in silence, willing her to go with her sister, but I saw the doubt in her eyes. More than that, I saw an inner struggle play out across her face.

She lowered her bag to the ground and turned to face Orpah. "I can't leave her," she simply said.

Orpah stared at Ruth, her mouth opening and closing as words came and left. After several minutes, she shook her head in sadness. Tears streamed down

Orpah's face as she grabbed Ruth in a hug. They had not been close as children or younger women. In many ways, the two were opposites of each other, but their life together with Mahlon and Kilion had proven to them both that their differences could not stop love and friendship from building between them.

Still, I knew Orpah didn't really want to go on to Judah. I guess Ruth knew that as well, which may have been that internal struggle I witnessed.

"I love you, Ru," Orpah said quietly, pressing her forehead to Ruth's. "You know I can't go with you. Ima is right. I will go find my mother's family and begin again." She paused and wiped her eyes as she stepped away from Ruth. "I will think of you often."

She looked at me, sadness in her eyes, but said nothing. Instead, she took the reins for the mule and turned to the road in the direction the merchant's caravan had gone. I watched her go and prayed she would catch up to the merchant's caravan.

Ruth watched her sister move farther and farther away from her. She sobbed openly before she turned and ran to me. I stood still as Ruth clung to me. Strong emotion caused my voice to tremble, "Ruth. Go. Orpah is returning to your people, to your gods. You should return with her. You can catch up with her and travel together. Go on."

Ruth gripped me even tighter and struggled against the sobs that wracked her body. She shook her head, denying my encouragement for her to leave. "Don't ask me to leave you or to turn back from following you because wherever you go, I will go. Wherever you live, I will live. Your people will be my people too, and your God will be my God. Wherever you die, I will die, and there I will be buried. Let the Lord kill me or worse if anything but death parts us."

I deflated within Ruth's embrace as it hit me that I could not talk Ruth into returning to her own people. Dread once again sat heavy in my gut as I realized the hardship the younger woman would likely face in Judah. It was one thing for me to return to Ephrathah alone, a widow with no sons. My life would be dependent on the kindness of relatives and strangers for the rest of my life. Among my people, I would likely be an outcast as well to some extent, but they were my people, and that mattered.

For Ruth, I knew, life would be much harder. No one would care that she had once been a princess. All they would see was that she was a Moabite and a widow. She would be cast out, ridiculed, maybe cared for grudgingly with scraps of scraps, but it was not likely she would find a suitable husband simply because of her own heritage.

I sighed heavily and pried Ruth off me. Ruth wiped her eyes and stared at me. Could she see the doubt in my eyes? The fear? The dread? I tried hard to compose myself, but the emotions were nearly overwhelming, so I turned away from her without a word. Behind me, she grabbed her bag and tied it to the mule, then she led the mule behind me while I led the way in silence.

PART TWO: RUTH

So the two women went on until they came to
Ephrathah. When they arrived in Ephrathah, the
whole town was stirred because of them,..
So Naomi returned from Moab accompanied by Ruth
the Moabite, her daughter-in-law, arriving in
Ephrathah as the barley harvest was beginning.
Ruth 1:19, 22

ONE

Naomi and I stared down at the sprawling town in silence. I looked down at Ephrathah with excitement and wonder. The town was not very big, but because of my father's reaction to it when he decided I should marry Mahlon, I assumed it was big enough to have rivaled the city I had grown up in. I was surprised but not disappointed. I watched the dots of people moving about the area around the town. There were plots of land green with crops, while there were others that were golden yellow–crops nearly ready for harvest. There were fresh smells of fruit, grain, and herbs in the air. I could hear children laughing and women singing.

I smiled widely. This was to be my new home!

I thought back over the past decade. My life as a princess had been full of wealth and ease, but it had been empty, devoid of something that I had never real-ized until I had met Mahlon. When I married him and had become part of his house, I found not only love with him but also unexpected love, friendship, and companionship from Naomi. I had learned a deep joy that even with all the hardship we faced, I would never trade for all the riches in the world. I stared at Naomi in all her sadness. With a startling realization, I saw that Naomi was still a woman of God; she was still a woman who loved, hoped, and prayed. Naomi had never stopped praying. I saw something in Naomi I did not fully understand, but it was something I admired and wanted to experience myself.

Naomi looked down at her home. While I felt excitement, Naomi appeared to be full of doubt and fear.

"Lord, help me," Naomi breathed quietly.

I glanced at her, not sure I heard her correctly. "Did you say something?"

The trip after Orpah left us had been awkward because Naomi simply stopped talking to me. Entirely. She didn't ask for help along the journey. She didn't tell me about Ephrathah. Naomi didn't talk to me, not even small talk. Every answer to any of my questions was clipped and as brief as possible. I didn't even hear Naomi say her prayers in the morning or at night. She acted as though she were mad at me, and I could not understand why.

Naomi ignored my question. She had to know her silence was hurtful to me.

I turned to face Naomi fully. "Have I upset you?" I asked bluntly, unable to take her sullenness any longer.

Naomi, tears welling in her eyes, shook her head that she was not upset with me. Before I could ask her anything else, Naomi moved ahead of me. She moved past me and toward Ephrathah. I shrugged. I trusted her to be honest with me, but I was troubled that she was so upset and refused to talk to me about it. Still, I followed behind her, and together we moved down the hill and into Ephrathah.

I felt eyes on us from the women gleaning in the fields. The men working on the tools or with the livestock didn't so much as glance at us, but the women all seemed to be very curious about the two of us.

Suddenly, one woman near the edge of one of the fields rushed up to Naomi.

"Naomi?" the woman asked. "Heavens, is that really you?"

She stared hard at Naomi, who simply stared back. The woman waved to all the other women in the fields.

"It's Naomi! Naomi has come home! Come! Come! Naomi is home!"

Shouts rose from the edges of the fields and then through the fields, and dozens of women ran to the road to see for themselves. Before long, a circle of women stood around us. They had to see how weary and worn out we were. They clearly noted the absence of Elimelek and Naomi's sons, but the women simply welcomed Naomi home. A few cast curious glances at me but didn't approach me. Maybe they thought I was Naomi's servant.

The woman who had run up initially turned to the gathered crowd of women, and called out, "Look! It is Naomi!"

Several of the women, not able to see her clearly, called back, "Is it Naomi? Really?"

I could hear the indistinct murmurs among the women. They were wondering where the men were. I knew they were curious, even wary of me standing behind Naomi. I stood still among the strangers, but Naomi took a deep breath and raised her hands to get the group's attention.

"Don't call me Naomi. Instead, call me Mara for the Almighty has dealt very bitterly with me. I went out full, and the Lord has brought me home again empty." She paused and I saw all the worry and stress she'd lived under suddenly appear on her face. How had I missed the depth of her pain all these years? I watched her take a deep breath and compose herself as she continued, "Why do you call me Naomi when the Lord has testified against me, and the Almighty has afflicted me?"

A hush settled over the gathered women as Naomi's words hung over them. We could all hear her grief and feelings of betrayal. I realized instantly that most of the women around me also knew that grief and had suffered through the same feelings of abandonment when they struggled through the famine, losing their own husbands, children, and loved ones to starvation. Each of them could empathize with Naomi's deep sadness. They understood why she felt abandoned by God. Still, they could look around in the aftermath of such sadness and see how He had blessed them.

One woman stepped forward and hugged Naomi tightly. "We know your pain, sister. But Yahweh remains. He brought you home to us, and He will see that you are blessed again. I believe that with all my heart."

Naomi stiffened in the woman's arms, but I could tell that the woman's words touched Naomi's heart. I watched her face and could see her walls fall. Tears streamed down Naomi's face as she clung to the other woman. She wept openly among the women while they touched her, sang joyful songs of her return, and prayed to God in thanks for returning her to them.

Meanwhile, I stood at the edges, touched deeply by the homecoming that I had been completely unprepared for. They largely ignored me, but I didn't mind. My mother-in-law finally appeared at peace, something I had never seen in her before. And for that, I felt joy in my heart. I lifted my eyes to the heavens and prayed sincerely to Yahweh, thanking him for a place to call home.

TWO

W e were ultimately led by the group of excited women to Naomi's home that she had shared with Elimelek before they left Ephrathah. After so many years of neglect, the home had fallen into disrepair, but the main room was dry and sound. Many of the women took care to help us unpack the mule and get settled for the night. When Naomi revealed that I was her daughter-in-law, not her servant, several of the women reacted unexpectedly: they responded to me as they would an outcast and quickly left our presence. A few other women, however, must have noted the way we cared for each other and the obvious affection that Naomi had for me, and they remained until their duties called them back to their own families.

Over the next several days, we found daily portions of bread, herbs, meat, and fresh skins of water to help sustain us. Both of us prayed and cried together over the generosity being shown to us, but Naomi finally opened up to me about her fears concerning our life among her people.

"My dear, we cannot hope that this generosity will continue on indefinitely. We will have to take care of ourselves. For me, I must find a way to make something that I can sell at the market. And you... you must find a husband."

Slicing the meat and cutting herbs to serve with the bread for our dinner, I set the food aside and started to object, but Naomi held up a hand to indicate she would not argue.

"No. No. You must. You're too young to remain here with me as I wither away into old age. You must first go out and glean from the fields so that you may meet my people, to get to know them, to understand them. They must get to know you. They must see that you are one of us now. That you have embraced not just us as your own but also our ways and our God."

I frowned, not sure I understood, but I had noted how different I was treated when I was with Naomi around town, versus when I was alone around town. The small community all knew I was a Moabite. And while Naomi had told as many as she could that I was one of them, most only saw me as an outsider.

After several minutes of silent thought, I asked, "Ima, do I just go to any field?"

I knew how to glean in the fields; I had done so in the fields Mahlon and Kilion had planted year after year. I was no stranger to that work, and I looked forward to being busy even if it was among people who might not want me there.

Naomi shrugged her shoulders as she reached for the bread to break it into smaller pieces. "There are a few relatives we could ask for help from, but only a couple have fields where you might find work. Actually, Elimelek does have one relative that I think used to have the largest fields. If that is still true, and considering how this region is doing now, you are most likely to get the best gleanings there, but because you are a Moabite, you will need to hang back even behind the widows and orphans. Do you understand?"

I nodded.

Naomi sat down with a huff and wrung her hands before her, her face wrinkled in sudden worry. "Oh. No. No, that won't do," she muttered to herself before she looked at me. "I can't allow you to go out there all alone."

I set aside the meat and herbs and I took Naomi's hands in my own, not understanding her sudden conflict. "Please, Ima, explain."

Naomi avoided my eyes, "You are a Moabite. Not one of us. You will be shunned. You will be considered less than the poorest woman, less than the humblest widow, less than the hungriest child. You could be a target... the men... if something happened to you." Naomi visibly shuddered. "No. You can't go."

I sat in silence letting her words sink in. As they rebounded in my head, I took a deep breath, forcing my own fears down. "Let me begin to earn our own food. Maybe I can find enough so we can make extra bread you can sell. Then maybe we can set aside enough so we can start to do some repairs around this house." I peered at her, my desire to be a help outweighing my fears. "Please, tell me this relative's name so I can go to his fields and glean there. And we will pray to Yahweh that I might find favor with this relative."

Naomi sighed heavily. "I'm not sure about this at all. After all, we've been back in Ephrathah for nearly a week, and none of Elimelek's relatives have dropped in or welcomed us back. To my knowledge, they have not been among those who sent food to help us. This is a heavy and disappointing blow. Even so, we have a roof over our head even if there is much work to be done. We have food every meal even it if is at the mercy of strangers. Above all, we're alive, and in light of what we have just so recently experienced, this is a miracle."

She stared at me. I simply wanted to help, but I was not eager to remarry. My love for Mahlon had been genuine and deep, much as Naomi's had been for Elimelek, but I was also practical. I knew as well as Naomi did that the only way we could truly survive was for me to find a husband. Though, I supposed, I didn't have to rush. Maybe gleaning in the fields would be enough to sustain us for a while.

Naomi smiled at me while I internally prayed that if Yahweh wanted me to remarry that it please be someone I could love as I loved Mahlon.

We turned away from each other to eat our meal in silence.

The following morning, Naomi helped me dress and gave me a length of rope to tie the gleanings to my back at the end of the day. She helped tuck stray strands of hair under my tichel and kissed me on the forehead.

"Now. His name is Boaz. I know his fields are south of town, but I don't remember exactly where. As you move among the other young women, ask them and they can tell you."

I nodded absently as I secured my belt more tightly around my waist, my thoughts ahead on what the day might hold for me.

Naomi continued, "Remember, the men will cut the barley. Then they will go back to pick up what they cut. They will wrap the cuttings to be carried to the storage barns. Only after they have completed wrapping their bundles can you go gather the gleanings. Do you understand?"

I smiled. "I understand. I cannot pick up as I did in our own fields."

Naomi bit her lip as she watched me move toward the door; she started to say something but hesitated.

"And one other thing. Make sure you are never alone with any of the men. Okay? Don't follow them into the barns or to the threshing floor. Only go inside if other women are with you. Otherwise, simply wait until they are finished if you need to go inside."

My mother-in-law smiled as I kissed her on the cheek. "I understand, Ima. I will do my best to be a hard and blameless worker. I won't do anything to bring our family shame."

With a nervous smile and a wave, I left Naomi standing in the doorway staring after me.

THREE

I wandered through Ephrathah and out the southern gates. As I left the town, the fields of golden barley stretched out before me on both sides of the packed dirt road. I adjusted my tichel and moved briskly down the road. I moved to the back of a small group of young women and listened to their conversation for a bit. Hoping to learn something of the town and the people, I was slightly put off that the women only seemed to be talking of the men that they fancied or hoped to catch the eye of.

One of the women noted my presence and turned to me as we walked. "You are the woman who came back with Naomi. Right?"

I nodded. "I am Ruth."

The woman smiled. "I am Jera. You are Naomi's servant?"

I glanced at the other women, who were listening intently, some watching me as they walked, clearly curious. I shook my head. "No. Not a servant. I was married to Mahlon."

Some of the women gasped and immediately started whispering among themselves. I overheard bits and pieces of what they were saying and my cheeks flushed red.

"Moabite."

"Heathen."

"Yahweh judged."

Jera grabbed my wrist and whispered. "Never mind them. We have strict ways, and sometimes, that causes us to be ugly to others when we should be welcoming."

I smiled at Jera. "Thank you."

Jera fell in beside me and the two of us let the other women walk ahead. "Do you mind if I ask what happened? It's been over ten years since Elimelek packed up and left. Most of us thought he and Naomi would be back in a year. It was quite shocking to see Naomi return alone, well, without Elimelek, Mahlon, and Kilion."

My chest tightened, and Jera noted my sudden discomfort. "Oh. Never mind. You don't have to tell me. After all, I'm a stranger to you. Instead, tell me, have you gleaned before?"

I nodded, shaking off my grief. "I am supposed to find the fields of Naomi's kinsman, but I don't have any idea how to do that."

Jera laughed. "Who is it?"

I responded, "I think his name is Boaz."

Jera nodded. "Of course. I think there are other kinsmen, but none have fields ready for harvest. I believe Boaz has a couple of barley fields. Come, I will take you."

I thanked Jera, and we continued to talk as we went, Jera filling me in on the rumors and happenings of Ephrathah. After a short while, Jera stopped at the edge of a field and waved over a middle-aged man. "Helon, can you use another woman to help with the gleaning?"

The man frowned at Jera. "You know we can, Jera. Why do you ask?"

Jera ignored his question and turned to me. "Ruth, this is my cousin, Helon. He manages the reapers for these fields. He will see that you know what to do."

She started to walk away, but I called out to her. "Wait. Aren't you staying?"

Jera laughed lightly. "Oh, no. I am taking my husband his lunch. He is a very forgetful man." She shrugged and smiled. "I hope to see you again, Ruth."

I smiled then turned to Helon who stood frowning at me. "Well, come along. You can wait over there with the other widows. Do I need to show you how to do it as well?" he asked huffily.

"No, sir. I know how."

"Good. Very good." Helon stopped and looked closer at me. "You are the woman who was with Naomi, yes?"

I smiled and nodded. "I am."

"Hmmm. I thought so. Well, fine, fine. Just stay out of the way of my reapers as well as the women who are binding the sheaths. Then double-check with me before you leave for the day. Do you understand?"

I confirmed that I did and went to join the women as they waited to bind or glean the barley after the reapers.

The sun had already passed its zenith and was well on its way to sunset as Boaz rode across his field in search of Helon. He rode past many of his workers, men and women alike, and called out a greeting to each of them as he passed.

"The Lord be with you," he called out, and the workers returned the greeting. Riding along the lines of men who were cutting the barley, he made sure that nothing was being missed. He looked behind the men and saw the wives and children gathering the cuttings and tying them into sheaths that would be picked up once the barley had dried and then moved to the threshing floors.

He smiled at the productivity of his people and praised God that they had a harvest to reap. It looked to be an overly abundant harvest. As he rode along, he noted the familiar faces and sadly noticed how many faces were missing. Most of the older men and women had not survived the famine, and many of the children had also died at the hands of starvation. Still, he noted that there were a few new faces among his people.

He stopped his horse as he noticed one young woman at the back of the group. He could not make out her face clearly, but he noted how diligently she worked, careful to pick up every scrap she could, making small bundles that she then tucked into her sack. She turned toward him but was still bent low over the ground. After a few moments, she stood up straight to stretch her back and roll her shoulders, and he saw her face clearly. She did not talk to anyone or take more than a few moments to stretch, and she bent back over and moved slowly after the women ahead of her.

Wondering who the woman was, Boaz spurred his horse onward, still greeting people as he passed until he stopped at a wagon where Helon was directing men from another field to gather the dried sheathes and take them to the threshing floor.

"The Lord be with you," Boaz greeted Helon.

Helon bowed his head and returned the greeting. "It is good to see you, Boaz."

"It is a beautiful day, isn't it, Helon? How goes it?"

Helon glanced out over the workers in the field. "We have a great harvest and enough men and women to gather. So far, we have had no problems. The crop seems healthy. We should be able to fill the stores for winter even after making sure each family takes home their earnings."

Boaz smiled at the good news. He looked back out over the field where most of the people were working and he caught sight of the unknown woman again.

"Helon, who is that woman over there? What family is she from? I don't recognize her."

Helon stood up on the back of the wagon and looked at where Boaz was pointing. "The one at the back?"

Boaz nodded.

"Oh. She is new. She is the young Moabite woman who came back with Naomi. She asked if she could glean after the reapers and among the sheaves. I agreed, and she has been working hard from early morning till now with only a short rest in the shack at the edge of the field."

"She came back with Naomi, Elimelek's wife?"

Helon replied, "It is rumored the young woman was married to Mahlon before he was murdered by the Moabites."

Boaz frowned. He did not begrudge Elimelek's leaving when he did in the midst of the famine, but it hurt his heart that all that remained of Elimelek's family was his wife and daughter-in-law. It was tragic.

He looked to Helon, "Be sure she is treated kindly. I will not tolerate any abuse shown her because of her nationality."

Helon frowned, "That might be hard, my lord."

Boaz stared at Helon, "See that she comes to no harm. Understand?"

Helon nodded, and Boaz rode over to where Ruth was working diligently.

She looked up as his horse approached and watched him hop from the saddle with ease. He approached her, and she bowed deeply before him. "My lord..." she began.

He interrupted, "Listen to me, young woman. Come back only to my fields to glean for the remainder of the season, and stay close to my men and women as they work. Keep your eyes open as they work, and follow them closely. I have given orders that the men won't harass you or abuse you so have no fear of them. If you get thirsty, help yourself to the water-skins and drink from what my men have drawn from the wells."

Ruth fell to her knees and pressed her head to the ground before Boaz. "What have I done that gained your notice and your mercy even though I am an outcast, a foreigner among your people?"

Boaz leaned down and gently helped her to her feet. He looked into her eyes and saw the kindness and sincere confusion there. "I have been told all that you have done for Naomi since the death of your husband. I know that you left your family and the land of your birth to follow Naomi to a people and a place you did not know before. I pray that the Lord will repay your work and give you full reward for seeking refuge under His wings."

Ruth choked out, "I hope I find favor in your sight, my lord, because you have given me comfort and have spoken kindly to me even though I am not one of your people."

Boaz saw her struggling to keep her composure and thought it best to leave her alone. He said nothing else, but instead got back on his horse and rode to where Helon waited with a wagon. From there, Boaz watched Ruth wipe her eyes and face, lift her face to the sky, and then bend back over the ground as she continued to work.

FOUR

fter my encounter with Boaz, I worked afresh until the sun was low over the horizon, casting the world in beautiful hues of gold. I stood up from my work and raised my arms over my head, stretching this way and that to get the tension out of my neck and shoulders. Smiling to myself, I took in the field I had been working in. The reapers and the women gathering together the sheaths had done a lot of work that day. Many of them were leaving the field and heading toward the low building where a fire was lit inside. Laughing and singing were coming from inside the building, but I didn't know what was going on, so I bent back to my work, not thinking anything of it.

I was caught off guard moments later when a woman approached me. "Are you Ruth?" she asked, hefting her sack on her hip awkwardly.

I nodded and smiled.

The woman nodded over her shoulder, "Boaz asked me to come to you, to make sure you are invited to join us for our evening meal and prayers. He insists."

I glanced behind the woman and saw Boaz watching us, but could not make out his expression. I set my sack down in the dirt so I would know where to start again after this gathering. Looking at the woman, I replied, "Thank you. I will follow you."

As we neared the low building, the woman bowed slightly before Boaz. "Thank you," he said to the woman, and she walked away, glancing curiously at us.

I bowed my head to Boaz. "You wanted to see me?"

Boaz nodded. "I did. Come. It is the time we gather together to praise our Lord for the harvest and eat together. Come sit with us, eat of our bread, and help yourself to the vinegar for your bread."

I followed behind Boaz in a daze not knowing how to react to this invitation. The other workers stopped eating as I followed behind their lord, and whispers arose as he sat down and directed me to sit beside him among the reapers.

Self-conscious of the stares that were focused on me, I sat down. I kept my eyes low, unable to meet the penetrating looks of the men around me and those of the women who sat beyond them.

Boaz took a loaf of bread, praying as he did so. I bowed my head, listening to Boaz's prayer and thinking one of my own. After he was done, he broke the bread and laid it on a platter, which he then handed to me.

He was honoring me by handing the platter of bread to me first. I bowed my head, not meeting his eyes, and I took the platter as though it were a holy object. Staring at the bread for a moment, I finally took a large piece and then passed the platter on to the man on the other side of me.

I ate my bread in silence while Boaz and the men spoke of the harvest and plans for threshing, flour making, and preparing the fields for the next sowing season. After just a short while, I had my fill but still had a large lump of bread so I tucked it away into my robes to share with Naomi at home.

As the men were in conversation, I rose to my feet and silently left the building. Still unsure of why I was invited to sit beside Boaz, thinking the man was incredibly kind, I returned to the field and my work.

After the meal, the men also returned to the fields. By the time the sun began to sink over the horizon, I had finished gleaning for the day. I moved to the corner of the field and beat the barley out of the grain I had picked up. I gathered it all together and put it in my sack.

Once I was done, I was happily surprised that I had gathered nearly an ephah, or bushel, of barley to take home to Naomi. I could not believe so much had been left behind. That was enough barley to feed us for a couple of weeks. We could make bread and rolls to sell or exchange for other things we needed.

I bowed my head and prayed to the Lord in thankfulness for the blessings He had bestowed on me, first by leading me to meet Jera, then finding me a place in Boaz's fields, and finally, for the abundance of grain for our meals.

Helon approached me. "It is good you are giving thanks, woman. Boaz is well-known for his generosity, but he has shown you more generosity than I have ever seen."

I stared at the man, waiting for him to continue as I wondered why he sought me out.

"The men ahead of you were told to deliberately leave more behind for you to pick up. Everything you carry from this field is a gift. I hope you understand just how favored you have been today."

I blinked rapidly, the revelation touching me deeply. Inwardly, I thought Boaz must be so generous because of Naomi. Not that it mattered, he had no reason to be this kind, and yet he was. I could tell Helon wasn't sure he approved.

I smiled up at Helon. "I thank Yahweh for Boaz's kindness. I promise I will earn whatever he deigns to allow me."

My response must have soothed Helon's fears. He nodded curtly and turned away from me. A few steps from me he turned back. "I assume you will return tomorrow?"

"Yes, if I may."

He glanced out over the fields, his lips in a thin line as he thought.

"Be sure to start on that far edge over there," he pointed. "The men will just be starting there tomorrow, which should prove to be a plentiful harvest for you."

Once again, tears stung my eyes, and I nodded mutely in understanding.

Without another word, Helon walked across the field to the road and began his own trek back toward town.

It was nearly dark when I finally saw the house and Naomi standing in the door waiting for me. I smiled to see her excitement at my return. She rushed out to meet me, astonishment on her face to see the bulk of the sack I carried.

Naomi reached out to take the sack from me, but I shook my head, suddenly weary from my hard day. I reached into my robes and pulled out the bread I had not finished and handed it to Naomi. She took it and felt its freshness, falling into step beside me as she tore off little bits of the bread and ate them.

"Tell me, child. Tell me everything. Whose field did you end up in? How did you end up with this much from gleaning? Whoever took notice of you be blessed! This is so much more than I expected!"

I nodded, bemused and excited even though I was exhausted. As we neared our home, I looked at Naomi. "I worked in Boaz's fields today."

Naomi breathed a sigh of relief. "Blessed be Boaz for following the Lord's will and not withholding his kindness to us. He is one of our closest relations. He must have realized that."

"He told me to only return to his fields for the remainder of the harvest. And…. Helon told me that Boaz directed the men ahead of me to leave more than they really should."

Naomi nodded and sighed happily. "That is good, daughter. Being among his women, being among his workers will keep you protected as you might not have been among other fields."

I nodded in agreement.

We walked together to the house in silence, each lost in our own thoughts and thankfulness.

FIVE

I woke long before sunrise the next morning. I stared up at the ceiling above me as the early morning light shone dimly through cracks in the roof Elimelek's extended family had kept the house standing but otherwise invested very little in keeping the home in repair. I had offered to climb up on the roof to patch the biggest holes, but Naomi insisted it was something she was capable of doing, saying she needed to drag mats to the roof anyway to further dry whatever I brought home from the fields. I let the matter lie but inwardly determined to be the one climbing the steep and narrow steps on the side of the house that led to the flat roof to lay the mats before Naomi had a chance.

I rolled onto my side and observed Naomi across the room, still asleep. My mother-in-law appeared to be sleeping more comfortably in the little time we had been back in Ephrathah than she had during our travels from Moab. Naomi's chest rose and fell in her slumber, and I felt sudden relief and gratitude that we had made the journey safely and that Naomi was once again in the place she had been praying to be for so long.

I smiled to myself and quietly got to my feet. Stepping past the thick blanket that separated the area where we slept from the rest of the main room where we also cooked, ate, and worked on our various chores, I tiptoed to a basin that had water in it. I fished out the few bugs that had found their way into the water during the night and splashed my face before unbinding my hair to brush it out. While I brushed my hair, I looked out a side window and watched the people already moving about on the dirt road that ran nearby. Mostly they were older children leading live-stock to graze on the hillsides although there were a few men and women already on their way to work in the fields. I rebraided my hair in a hurry and then pulled a tichel, a wool strip of cloth that I tucked my hair into, over my head. Grabbing my mourning cloak, I threw it over my loosely belted halug and rushed out the door. Hoping my rush didn't wake Naomi, I lifted one of three heavy woven mats to my shoulder and began climbing up the narrow steps to the roof.

On the roof I stepped lightly, unsure the roof was safe to be standing on. Carefully, I unrolled the mat across the roof before I went back down for the next one and then the last one. Once I was finished unrolling the third mat on the roof, sure to place it over the area we slept below, I stood up and stretched, taking in the rest of the roof that was broken, cracked, and had holes throughout. From my vantage point, I could see neighboring rooftops with their own mats for drying grains and herbs. Many other rooftops also had little tents set up, complete with thicker mats and pillows for lounging.

I sighed in sudden unbidden regret as I remembered the home I shared with Mahlon. I missed the grandness of it. It was far larger than this house, and it had always been maintained. Every room held a lifetime of memories, good and bad. There had been love, and I felt a sudden longing for it. My chest tightened as memories of Mahlon washed over me, and my eyes burned from the tears that threatened to spill over.

Glancing at the road, I noted more people were heading along it toward the fields, and I knew I needed to be on my way. I went down the stairs and into the house where I found Naomi, clearly just wakened, staring at me from behind the hanging blanket.

"Were you just up on the roof?" Naomi asked.

I grinned and hugged Naomi. "Boker tov! Yes. The mats are up there and laid out."

Naomi playfully swatted at me. "Child, I told you I would get them! What if you fell through?"

Giving Naomi a mock gasp of horror, I stepped away from the older woman and threw up my hands in exasperation. "I probably would have been fine. You, on the other hand..."

Naomi stepped toward the water basin to wash her face, commenting as she went, "You better get a bite to eat and be on your way, my dear."

I nodded and reached for a handful of dates, then tucked a couple of cloth sacks into my belt. I pecked Naomi on the cheek, and without a word, rushed out the door toward Boaz's fields.

~

I reached the field I had worked the day before just in time to see Jera turn away from her husband, who was already getting to work. Seeing Jera, I smiled widely.

"*Shalom!*" I called to the other woman.

Jera returned my smile and walked toward me. "I heard your first week went well in Boaz's fields," Jera commented.

I felt the color rise in my cheeks and bit my lip. "Yes. He was unexpectedly kind to me."

Jera reached out and patted me on the shoulder. "Nonsense. My husband commented that you work harder than all the other women combined. That said, be mindful of the other women. They can be catty and jealous sometimes, especially when someone else's hard work is rewarded while their own laziness is not."

I shook my head. "Are you telling me to do less?"

"Oh, no!" laughed Jera. "Absolutely not! You do whatever you need to do. I am simply passing on what my husband observed so you aren't caught off guard if the other women seem a little distant."

"Well, they have been, but I just assumed it was because... because I am a Moabite."

"That is part of it, for certain, but ..." Jera's comment faded to nothing and she shook her head. "Never mind. I am coming back during the noon meal, so I will see you then?"

I nodded with a smile and watched Jera leave the field and head back to Ephrathah. Turning back to the field, I noted several women watching me while the men were already hard at work cutting the tall stalks. Ignoring the stares, I stepped in line behind one of the men and began my own work, bending low over the ground gathering what I could.

Steps crunched on the drying stalks on the ground, and a shadow fell on the ground ahead of me. Out of the corner of my eye, I saw a water-skin being held out to me. Without looking, I gathered stalks from the ground and added them to my bundle. I shook my head. "No. Thank you."

The shadow shifted and fell across my face. "Come now, you must have some water. Have you had a break yet today?"

I suddenly recognized Boaz's voice. I stood up straight, my face twisted in a grimace as pain jolted across my lower back from hours of bending over with no rest. Putting my hands to my back to rub the sore area, I looked up at Boaz who stood with his arms still outstretched with the skin in one hand and the open top in the other where a small cup hung from it on a leather tie.

I smiled at Boaz and nodded. Reaching out, I took the cup in my hand, and Boaz lifted the water-skin until water poured into the small cup. Drinking the cool water quickly, I let the empty cup fall from my hand. As it swung freely, I met Boaz's gaze, and I bowed my head slightly.

"Thank you."

Boaz popped a top onto the skin and looked around the field, watching everyone hard at work. Then he turned his attention back to me. "Did you glean enough yesterday for yourself and Naomi?"

"Yes. Thank you."

"My foreman tells me that you worked very hard yesterday, and he reports that this morning, you are doing the same."

Embarrassed to be noticed, I ran the corner of my tichel over my face, wiping the sweat and dirt knowing that I was probably leaving smudges along my cheeks. I suddenly felt small under Boaz's scrutiny and wondered if I had overstepped in some way.

I started to apologize, but Boaz continued, "You are doing very well here. My offer remains. You are welcome to remain working in my fields through the rest of the harvest season."

I held my tongue between my teeth. I had to stop myself and gather my wits before I responded. This repeat offer was much more than I could have hoped for. Boaz had already shown me so much kindness. For him to retain me for the rest of the harvest was remarkable. From Jera, I learned that most landowners preferred that widows and orphans only remain in their fields a short time, often going out of their way to shoo them off if they returned too often.

"Of course. I will return so long as I gain favor in your sight."

Boaz said nothing but looked away for a few minutes watching the workers then glancing up again at the clouds in the sky. I watched him, taking in his bearing and demeanor. Boaz was clearly older than me by many years. He wore his dark hair short, his beard long. The skin on his face, arms, and hands was darkly tanned with almost a reddish tone to it. His dark eyes were bright and kind, laugh lines crinkling the corners. When he spoke, he had straight white teeth that showed he cared for himself. He stood tall, taller than Mahlon, and he was broader in the shoulder too.

What it would feel like to be in his embrace?

At that moment, Boaz returned his attention to me, and I immediately looked away, a light flush touching my cheeks.

"A storm is gathering, I think. I understand you and Naomi are residing in their home, not with relatives?"

I nodded. "We are."

"But the home is in disrepair, is it not?"

I shrugged my shoulders. "It is still standing, and we are only using the spaces that are still in livable condition."

"But the roof... By now, it must need some repair."

Suddenly unsure of how much to tell Boaz, I bit my lip before responding. "It's true. There are some holes and cracks in the roof. But just this morning, I covered them with thick mats..."

Boaz glanced up at the sky and clucked his tongue. "Mmm... That won't do. Come along."

Without another word, he turned toward the front of the field where his wagon waited. I fell in behind him and followed as he nearly trotted to Helon. "Helon, gather three or four of the men and take Ruth to Naomi. See that Elimelek's house has a repaired roof before that storm rolls in."

Helon stared at me, and then looked at Boaz, "We may not be able to fix the entire roof in time, if at all..."

Boaz waved the older man's objection away. "Go see what needs to be done. Then do what you can. If it looks as though the structure will not be waterproof because it can't be repaired in time, then please see that

Naomi and Ruth are taken to my sister's for the duration of the storm."

Helon did not waste any time. Calling out for four men, he waited for them to gather about him before directing them to follow along while he helped me onto the wagon and climbed up beside me.

The bundle on my lap, I looked down at Boaz with tears in my eyes. "Naomi... I... How do we thank you for...?" Then I looked at the bundle on my lap, "I haven't turned this in..."

Boaz shook his head. "You take that home to Naomi and tell her Boaz sends his greetings and his blessings. Come back after Sabbath to continue your work."

I nodded, unable to even utter thanks, as Boaz's kindness washed over me and caused me to tear up in gratitude.

As Helon moved the wagon back toward Ephrathah, I looked over my shoulder to see Boaz staring after us.

SIX

I wiped my brow as I rested under the canvas of the temporary shelter placed to the side of the last field to be harvested. I could feel the sweat running down my back, and I shrugged in my halug as the sensation tickled. With a slight smile on my face even as exhaustion threatened to overtake me, I focused my gaze on the people in the field.

After two months of working in Boaz's fields, I had come to know many of the men and women I worked alongside. I reflected on how they had ignored me, how they ridiculed me after Boaz appeared to favor me, a Moabite and a widow. That had been true at first. I did not blame them. My time among the people of Ephrathah had taught me much about them, their culture, and their faith. The more I learned, the harder I worked to gain their trust and hoped to earn a modicum of acceptance.

As I sipped at a cup of water and watched the others, I believed I was gaining that desired acceptance. I knew so many of the other women by name now. Some had shared their lunches with me. Others had included me in conversation and gossip. A few, like Jera, had invited me and Naomi over for Sabbath multiple times and occasionally checked in on the two of us to make sure there was nothing we needed.

Even Boaz, much to the increased gossip of the women, stopped by to check on me. Jera dismissed my concerns assuring me that Boaz's visits were out of a sense of duty per the customs of his people, but the more I was around the mature man, the more I felt drawn to him and sensed he was also drawn to me.

"Yahweh. Please... remove these feelings if they are not of your design. Guard my heart and lead it elsewhere," I whispered into the stillness of the shelter.

"What was that?" interrupted a masculine voice and I found myself both jumping and blushing at being startled in my solitude and prayer. I turned to face Boaz as he stepped to the edge of the shelter without moving under its protective shade, a clear sign of respect and etiquette.

I bowed my head. "Shalom. I didn't know there was anyone about."

I hoped he didn't notice the rising color in my face, but he turned away from me though as he continued to address me. "You do know you can go with Naomi to the temple to offer your prayers. You don't have to say them out here in the fields."

I shrugged my shoulders. "Naomi isn't comfortable taking me to the temple. She fears I have not been accepted yet and that if I go it may cause trouble. Besides, I enjoy talking to Yahweh here in the fields. On the long days, talking to Him helps the time pass, and in a lot of ways, helps me work through things in my mind."

Boaz turned to me, his eyebrows raised as he stared at me. He must have thought me very strange. After all, I was not of his people. I hoped I hadn't overstepped my bounds by sharing my longing for Yahweh.

Growing uncomfortable under Boaz's scrutiny, I lifted my shawl over my head and stepped into the sunlight. "I, um, should get back to work."

Boaz raised a hand to stop me. "Today will see the end of the harvest. Have you and Naomi enough to get you both through the next several months?"

I heard the concern in Boaz's voice. Genuine care. My heart warmed to him and I nodded in response.

"I think so. Naomi and I have been taking half of everything you have allowed me to take home and have done what we can to preserve it for the coming months. With the other half, we have baked and cooked and sold what we can to add coin to our savings, keeping only what we need to eat. Naomi is teaching me a great deal about how to plan for the lean months and how a single coin can be used to purchase several times its worth. She is very smart about such things."

Boaz smiled as he looked out over the fields. "That is good to hear. I worry about the two of you."

I bowed my head in response. "No need to worry. Yahweh provides."

Boaz looked at me and I hoped he knew I meant what I said. Before he let me return to my work, he asked me, "Do you happen to know if *Tov* has visited with Naomi?"

"Tov, my lord?"

Boaz frowned. "You do not know Tov?"

I shook my head and squinted up at Boaz. "I don't believe so. Why would he see Naomi?"

Boaz frowned even deeper. Was that anger I saw flitting across his features?

Looking at me, he forced a smile to his lips. "No matter. I was simply wondering. Shalom, Ruth. After today and the work is all complete, please, do not hesitate to reach out if you and Naomi are in need of anything.

I bowed slightly before Boaz and nodded my thanks then I turned on my heel, confused by this exchange with him. As I moved behind the lines of men and women threshing and gathering, my thoughts remained on the strange question. Who was this Tov? I resolved to ask Naomi once I got home.

SEVEN

I entered the home to find it dark and empty. Setting my bag on the table, I called Naomi's name as I moved to the windows and pushed aside the heavy fabric, letting the dim light of sunset illuminate the room behind me until I could light the oil lamp. Once the lamp was lit, I carried it through the other rooms of the house in search of Naomi, only to realize that my mother-in-law was nowhere to be found. Assuming Naomi must have gone to the market before all the shopkeepers closed up for the evening, I returned to the main room. I hung the oil lamp from a hook that dangled over the table and turned to my bag. I removed the remnants I had gathered that day and laid them to the side to take care of the next day.

After I cleared the table, I noted that Naomi had made bread earlier that day, so I took the bread to the table and cut it into thick slices. Then I rummaged about the shelves under the window and found some wilted herbs from the day before, a small flask of wine, and some dried meat. Setting it all neatly on the table along with some clay plates, I went to the door and stood waiting for Naomi.

While I waited, leaning in the doorway, I again watched the people moving along the street. Among the faces I now recognized, I was delighted as a few said hello as they passed while others simply nodded their heads in acknowledgment of my presence. I couldn't help but wonder if maybe I was finally being accepted by Naomi's people. Turning my attention to the gathering night, I watched as the stars began to twinkle in the darkening night sky. Staring up at them, I thought of a song that Naomi had taught me, and I hummed the melody to myself.

Several minutes later, I heard laughter from down the street and watched in curious wonder as I saw Naomi walking slowly home accompanied by two older children. As they got closer, I realized they were Jera's oldest children, and I moved to greet them.

"Shalom, Ima. Shalom, children."

I hugged Naomi and noted the bundle she was carrying, so I gathered the bundle to myself, allowing Naomi to walk freely.

"What have we here?" I asked as I noted the weight and size of the bundle.

"Mama made you both some new halugs and robes!"

I stared down at the child, a young girl, nearly a teenager, and smiled in surprise. "She didn't!"

The girl smiled widely and nodded excitedly.

Then the girl's brother, a year older, held out his hands and showed me that he was carrying a basket also from Jera.

"Oh! What have you there?" I asked, my eyes wide as I exchanged a look with Naomi, who simply smiled and let the kids share. "Mama said we had too much fish, and I agree. I am so tired of eating fish. It's so salty and dry..."

Naomi chuckled, "Now, now, Silas. Salty dry fish is better than no fish at all, is that not so?"

The boy looked down at the ground and nodded. "Maybe. Still," he smiled up at me, "I am happy you are getting so much of it!"

Realizing we had made it to the house, we stepped inside, Naomi taking the basket of fish from the boy. "Thank you for walking me home, children. Please tell your mother that we will return this cloth and the basket tomorrow sometime."

The little girl shook her head. "No. No. Mama said that you were to have those as well."

I knelt down before the girl and hugged her tight even as I smiled warmly at the boy. "Please tell your mother that we are very grateful. Now run along. I am sure Jera has your meal waiting for you."

Without waiting, both children turned toward home and ran back, yelling at the other over who would make it home first.

I turned toward Naomi, who was smiling after the children. "Shall we eat too?"

Naomi met my gaze and nodded.

We sat and shared a prayer over the food before we began to eat. I shared with Naomi that it was my last day in the fields, so I would be home to bake bread and help mend clothing or help with small repairs around the house. All the while, Naomi responded absently, nodding her head but not interacting with me.

I sat back and waited for Naomi to realize that silence had settled over the room. Finally, Naomi looked up from her food.

"I'm sorry, my dear. What was the last thing you said?"

I smiled back. "I have one question for you, and then I want to hear about your day."

Naomi took a piece of bread and waved at me to continue.

"Boaz asked me if Tov had talked to you. I don't know who that is, and Boaz didn't elaborate. Who is Tov, Ima? Should I know him? Boaz seemed upset that I didn't know..."

Naomi shook her head. "Tov is one of my husband's brothers. Before we left for Moab, Elimelek left his land in the care of his brother. He is our closest relative, and as he holds the land and because of our customs, he should have come to see me about his responsibility to me."

I frowned. "Responsibility to you?"

Naomi nodded. "It is complicated, my dear. We can discuss it some other time. But if Mahlon were alive, we would not live as we are, dependent on the kindness of Jera and our neighbors. We'd have fields of our own to tend to. We'd be able to help other families put food on their own tables. As it is... I am surprised Tov has not come yet, but then I suppose he is a busy man."

I sat in silence for a few minutes, not understanding why her husband's brother mattered. We could not even try to take the land back. As far as I was aware, that wasn't possible; women didn't own land or property in Judah. Thoroughly confused, I shook my head and shrugged.

"You were laughing as you were coming home. Ima, I have missed your laughter. It's so nice."

Naomi glanced at me and smiled warmly. "I was at the market trying to sell the loaves I made today, but we are not the only destitute women in Ephrathah right now. So many have lost their husbands, sons, daughters —their livelihoods. I just didn't have the heart to compete with those women who have children at home who need so much more than we do. So I divided the loaves up and gave them to some of those women—

more for them to sell—hopefully, more for them to take home to their families."

"Oh, Ima... that... is..." I felt such pride and love for Naomi. The words stuck in my throat as tears pricked at my eyes.

Naomi shook her head. "It is only right."

She paused as she took a bite of the dried meat and chewed on it for a few minutes, then she continued, "As I was leaving the market, I ran into Jera. I didn't realize she had seen what I had done, but she was rather outrageous about praising me for it. As she was gushing over me, some of my oldest friends overheard, and they came over to talk with me. In the end, we were invited to some of the ladies' homes for dinner sometime. Then Jera insisted I walk home with her because she had something, those clothes, I suspect, for you. Once I got there, I realized she had clothes for both of us and that basket of fish."

Naomi paused, wiping a tear from the corner of her eye. "Really, that Jera is entirely too generous."

I smiled and agreed.

We fell into a thoughtful silence as we reflected on our day. I thought of Jera's generosity, Naomi's selflessness, and of Boaz's concern for me and Naomi. While those things were to be counted as blessings, my other thoughts shifted to Tov and his apparent lack of concern, as was his duty, versus Boaz's obvious care and concern, and I prayed inwardly, "My Lord God, help me forward. Help me understand these things that are so foreign to me. Whatever causes Naomi and Boaz concern about Tov, Lord, please bring it to satisfaction."

EIGHT

I rose early and smiled into the shaft of sunlight that shone through the window and across my face. As I stared up at the repaired roof, courtesy of Boaz and Jera's husband, I moved to my knees and began to recite the prayers Naomi was teaching me. I smiled to myself as I recited the words, taking each one to heart, for I knew that God had something extraordinary planned for the people of Ephrathah.

Naomi had raised an eyebrow at me when I shared my thoughts that had come out of nowhere during my prayers the day before. The thoughts were a sort of promise that everything would be okay, that whatever hardships we were facing now would all come to an end. The results of all the hardships we had faced would bless not just us but all of Ephrathah, even Judah and Israel!

Yahweh was impressing that sense of hope in my heart and mind, and even as Naomi fretted constantly over our meager meals and constant struggle, I just grew more and more hopeful. Once I was finished with my morning prayers, I joined Naomi, who, as usual, was already awake and making our morning meal.

"Boker tov," I greeted quietly as I sat next to Naomi and helped divide a piece of flatbread.

Naomi smiled warmly. "It is a good morning, is it not?"

I nodded and glanced out the window. There were few people on the streets now that harvest was over. Now only the men reported to the threshing floors, getting the grain ready for storage for the long winter months. Most of the men typically left before the sun even rose, so the early morning streets were still and quiet, minus the few stragglers who woke late or had other business to attend to.

I jumped as Naomi took my hand. "My dear, I have a plan."

I looked at my mother-in-law as confusion knotted my gut. "A plan for what?"

"A plan for you. For your future," Naomi smiled and shrugged her shoulders, a sheepish look on her face, "and well, a plan for me as well."

I sat back and waited for Naomi to continue.

"We've been waiting for Tov to come do his duty to you and me both. I didn't explain all this to you, and I know you will find it disconcerting, but the truth is Tov should have come to offer to take you as his wife. In doing so, you'd be given the opportunity to bear an heir to Mahlon."

I felt my face heat in surprise and anger, "I cannot bear Mahlon an heir! This is absurd…"

Naomi raised her hand and waited for me to fall silent, but in my gut, I wanted to rail against what I was hearing. It made no sense.

Naomi continued, "Among our people, in order to keep family lines progressing, if the patriarch dies before an heir is born, the man's closest male relative is duty-bound to give the widow a son who would inherit the titles and property of the deceased. As our closest living kinsman, that is Tov's duty."

Naomi paused, and I tried to keep the frown from my face that would surely reflect my reluctance to even think about marrying the elusive Tov.

Naomi must have seen the disgust on my face. What a strange custom! To marry a man, bear children, and then those children would not be considered his? Among my people, that would never work. Besides, this Tov clearly had no interest in either of us. As Naomi resumed talking about Tov, I began to understand why: according to Naomi, Tov already had a wife and several children.

Even though my own father had many wives and even more children, after embracing Mahlon's lifestyle and his God, I could not help but feel as though multiple wives in one home, and one solely to help carry on another part of the family name, was somehow intrusive and even unsettling. I had a hard time trying to imagine how Tov's own wife might feel about the whole situation. Maybe his wife was the reason why Tov avoided us. Still, Tov had no excuse under their laws. He should have come to take me as his wife as well. And that also explained some of Boaz's questions, which also caused me some alarm. He knew of Tov's duty to me?

Naomi took a deep breath, noting my silence. "I understand why you hesitate. I would be hesitant too. But after praying over this ever since you told me Boaz asked about Tov, the Lord has impressed a plan on me."

She leaned in close to me, a twinkle in her eyes. "Now you must listen closely because if you don't do exactly what I say, this will cause harm to come to you instead of good. Worse, it could bring shame to Boaz, and after all he has done for us, for you, that is the last thing we want. But in Yahweh's name, you must be bold."

Intrigued, I leaned toward Naomi, looking deeply into her eyes. "Okay. I'm curious. What is your plan?"

Naomi smiled brightly as though it was the simplest plan in the world. "Now come along. You need to bathe well and anoint yourself with your perfumed oils. Put on your Sabbath clothes. You are going to visit Boaz. Tonight."

NINE

I stood in the shadows of the shelter where I had shared dinner with Boaz's men and women when we were still harvesting. Now, post-harvest, only the men remained in the fields here. As I waited, I hoped none of them would notice me, or if they did, that they would not recognize me. I waited until all the others had gone; the men leaning heavily on one another after hours of drinking wine with Boaz. I watched the men disappear from sight then turned and watched as Boaz grew more and more tired under the influence of the wine. I watched as he moved to the far end of the enclosed shelter where he laid down and closed his eyes. Before long, he was snoring, but still I waited for dark to completely settle over Ephrathah. I knew Naomi was home praying diligently and would likely stay awake and on her knees until I returned home, whenever that might be.

Lifting my eyes to the heavens, I prayed inwardly. *Oh God. Is this madness? Is this really what you want me to do?*

I don't understand how this can help us. I don't understand why you would want me to risk everything after we have already experienced small blessings in so many ways. Lord, if this is not what you want of me... If Ima is mistaken... Lord, I can't bring shame to Naomi. I can't bring embarrassment to Boaz.

As I thought of Boaz, my heart began to race in my chest. What would he think of me? If Naomi was wrong about this, Boaz could very well make our poor lives a living hell. Just the thought of raising his ire against me made chills run up and down my spine. I didn't want him to think poorly of me, but I wanted to be obedient to Yahweh. If Naomi was indeed inspired by the Lord, then I knew deep inside I could not turn away from this strange task.

I remained in the shadows, praying and pleading with God even as my fears and doubts threatened to overwhelm me. With my back against the rough walls of the shelter, I wrung my hands together and worked to keep my breathing steady. I prayed over and over for the Lord to help me, keep me safe, and guide my steps.

Finally, as the crescent moon rose higher and higher into the sky and as Ephrathah grew quieter and quieter in the night, I stepped out of the shadows and toward the entrance.

Naomi had learned from some of the townspeople that Boaz often slept in the threshing room until all the grain had been worked and gathered for storage. With a rash of thefts among grain stores as the people still bore the scars of the still too famine, many landowners chose to sleep among their grain stores until the grain could be processed and secured. It was well known Boaz did the same; he spent his evenings with his workers and then would simply remain there after all the others had gone.

I stared into the low building and took a deep breath. Naomi had insisted I bathe and dab on the perfumed oils Mahlon had once given me. She had also insisted I wear my nicest clothes. I objected at first. Dressing my best. Cleaning myself. Donning my perfume. Adding adornments. And then walking through Ephrathah at dusk. Lingering after dark? If I were seen, I'd immediately be considered a harlot.

Instead, I bathed and perfumed myself. Then I put on clean clothes and tucked my jewelry and my Sabbath clothes in a sack. Now that everyone was gone and with Boaz quiet inside, I shrugged out of my work halug and robe. In the deep shadows, I dressed in my finest and slipped on my jewelry. I rolled my other clothes into the sack. Anxiously, I stared out at the road and toward Ephrathah making sure no one had seen my transformation.

Lord, be with me, I prayed as I slipped through the wide doorway and stood with my back pressed against the wall just inside, waiting for my eyes to adjust to the darkness.

I stared about the large room and made out the low piles of grain, some threshed waiting to be put into bags and some still needing to be threshed. I noted the small table that held a pitcher and a plate with fruit on it as well as a lamp that had been used for lighting the room during the dinner. I inched my way along the wall of the building until I stood over the sleeping man.

Staring down at Boaz, I felt my heart begin to race again. In that instant, I prayed with all my heart that I was doing the right thing because I cherished the growing relationship I had with this man and feared that my actions might ruin that relationship. Unbidden, a tear streamed down my face. Wiping it away, I made sure to look around the room once more to make sure Boaz was alone. Taking a deep breath once I confirmed the fact, I knelt down at Boaz's feet. Feeling the thick edge of his mat, which stretched several inches beyond the length of his body, I carefully uncovered his feet and lay down below them.

Fully expecting my movements to waken the man, I lay perfectly still for several minutes expecting surprise, outburst, outrage, accusation. But Boaz continued to sleep, his breathing even and undisturbed. Lying on my side, my back to Boaz's feet, I listened to his breathing. Before long, my breathing matched his and peace settled over me.

Lord, please, your will be done was the last thing I remembered as sleep washed over me.

TEN

I sat up suddenly, a hand on my shoulder, gently shaking me. Blinking in the darkness, I saw it was still dark outside. Suddenly afraid, knowing I had been found, I turned my head to see who had been shaking me. Kneeling beside me, his hand now on his knee, was Boaz, staring at me intently. I felt the blood rush into my face and looked away quickly, the silence in the room deafening.

Finally, Boaz cleared his throat, breaking the silence.

"Who are you?" he asked, sleep heavy in his voice, and I realized it was too dark for him to make me out clearly.

"Ruth," I replied, my voice shaking with sudden sad dread, but I determined to obey Naomi and trust God, so I continued, "Spread your robe over your handmaid because you are a redeeming kinsman."

I heard him inhale sharply, before he shuffled backward and sat on the ground beside me.

"Ruth," he repeated softly, disbelief clear in his voice, "I know you are foreign, but do you understand what you just asked of me?"

Tucking my feet under me, smoothing my halug and robe out over my legs and knees, I turned slightly to look at Boaz. I knew, and I was terrified of his reaction once I revealed that I was fully aware.

"I can explain," I replied in barely a whisper.

Boaz said nothing. He simply sat and waited for me to elaborate.

Growing even more nervous under his steady gaze, I looked down at my hands. Thankful that it was still very dark to hide the heat in my face, I took a deep breath. "Naomi told me... She said I should come to you."

"In the middle of the night?"

"Yes," I said helplessly. It was complete madness. I knew it deep down. Coming to a man in the middle of the night. And I was a no one. I had nothing. I was nothing. I bowed my head, tears threatening to spill out of my eyes.

Boaz coughed, getting my attention. "Ruth, I don't understand. Why would Naomi tell you to do this? She is no stranger to our customs, our ways. What is her motive? Why would she tell you to do something so... dangerous?"

I clasped my hands tightly, willing myself to speak calmly and clearly. "Well... I found favor in your eyes, and I don't deserve it. I am not one of you, your people. Yet you have shown me kindness. You have gone out of your way to be sure Naomi and I both are cared for, wanting for nothing."

Boaz nodded, but remained quiet.

"Naomi told me I must remarry. I must marry a kinsman. Because of your kindness... because you are a relation... she hoped.... she hoped you would act on our behalf," I stuttered, suddenly unsure. This all felt so strange to say out loud. "I trust Naomi even if I am not certain of the strangeness of your people's customs. So, yes, I am asking you to cover me with your robe. I am asking you to take me as your wife."

I took a deep breath and prayed inwardly for God's guidance, starting to continue, but Boaz interrupted me. "May Adonai bless you. Your latest kindness is even greater than your first in that you didn't go after young men, neither rich ones nor the poor. And now, Ruth, don't be afraid."

Boaz sat back but reached out and took my hand. He squeezed it gently, and I felt sudden reassurance. He knew full well the risk I had taken. It was clear that he was shocked Naomi suggested it. As I sat there trembling with anxiety, I hoped he saw me for who I was. A woman widowed too young. One not afraid of hard work. Not afraid of being the outcast. Loyal to her mother-in-law. Loyal to her new God. And also a woman with a whole life ahead of her. A woman ready to start new. A woman who genuinely cared for him.

He broke into my thoughts. "I will do for you everything you say for all the city leaders among my people know that you are a woman of good character. It is true that I am a redeeming kinsman, but Tov is a closer relative than I am. Stay tonight. If in the morning, he will redeem you, fine! Let him redeem you. But if he doesn't want to redeem you, as Adonai lives, I will redeem you. I will make you my wife and fulfill the law so the line of Elimelek, the line of Mahlon, may continue on."

"Boaz?" I began, my voice shaking with unexpected emotion, but he raised a hand to quiet me.

"Now, lie down until morning."

I stared at Boaz, my heart plummeting even as I berated myself. Of course, he would think of Tov. That was the custom. That was the law. Still... I shook my head to get the unbidden thought from continuing, but it did anyway: I had hoped Boaz would... what? I thought to myself in frustration. Love me? Confess his undying devotion? Go against the traditions of his people? He was not Mahlon.

Still, he did say he would redeem me if Tov chose not to. That offer made me pray hard that the Lord's choice would be Boaz. As I lay back down, Boaz covered me with his robe. I was aware that he remained sitting, watching, and waiting. As we waited for dawn to come, I wondered if he could be affected by confronting Tov.

Would that confrontation come at a cost? I prayed that the Lord would give him the right words and that the Lord would be present and lead both men to act according to His will.

I must have fallen back asleep because I was jolted awake when Boaz once again lightly shook my shoulder. As I blinked my eyes open, I saw his face clearly - kind and open. He was close, and he smiled slightly as he brushed some hair from my face.

"Ruth, it is getting light. You must return to Naomi before the sun rises. No one must see you out this early."

I rose to my feet and looked down at Boaz.

"But..."

Boaz got to his feet as well and moved to stand in front of me. He stared down at me, his eyes boring into mine as though he were trying to fathom my thoughts. He reached out and replaced another errant strand of hair behind my ear, his hand lingering at the side of my face longer than it should have. Suddenly Boaz stepped back, clearing his throat.

"I will take your case before the elders at the gate. Tov will be there. I will see that he does right by you. For you. For Naomi. For Elimelek."

My eyes burned with building tears and my heart tightened as I realized that I didn't want Tov. I wanted Boaz. I wanted this man who treated me kindly. This one who treated me with respect. This one who treated me as though he had known me his whole life. This one I felt safe with. I turned my face away from Boaz so he could not see the tears brimming.

"Before you go, bring the shawl you are wearing and take hold of it."

I did as he asked, and Boaz surprised me by measuring six measures of barley into it.

"Thank you. You do us a great honor," I replied, my voice barely a whisper as I processed his continued generosity.

Boaz started to reach out to me, but he pulled his hand back and clasped his hands behind his back. Seeing the movement and praying inwardly that I wasn't being too forward, I stepped close to him and wrapped my arms around him.

I squeezed tightly, breathing in his scent, drawing on his presence and strength, but didn't wait for him to return my embrace. I just hoped my affection for him was felt in that embrace. I feared I may never be able to embrace him again after today.

His voice shook as he spoke, "Go, Ruth. Go now. And hurry. I will bring you word after I have had the meeting."

I nodded, and without another glance, I rushed across the room and out of the building.

ELEVEN

W e stared down at the open shawl with the six measures of barley spread on top. Naomi shed silent tears while I wrapped my arms around myself tightly, my mind and heart in turmoil as the sun rose outside.

"Tell me again what he said?"

I responded, "He said to me, 'You shouldn't return to your mother-in-law with nothing.'"

Naomi shook her head. "No. No. About Tov."

I rose to my feet and began to pace around the room. "I think I need to go for a walk," I said and started to go to the door.

Naomi rose and stopped me with a hug. "My daughter, just stay where you are until you learn how the matter comes out; Boaz won't rest until he resolves the matter today."

I stared into Naomi's face and nodded as I hugged her back. "I will try."

Together, we turned our attention back to the barley and then began to prep it for baking, cooking, and storage.

~

Across town, Boaz was already on his way to the city gates. He moved through Ephrathah with brisk purpose, readying himself to confront Tov on Ruth and Naomi's behalf. As he walked, he greeted others as they went about their business. Finally, he approached the gates and took a seat among the other men.

"Boker tov, Boaz. It is a fine morning," greeted one of the older men.

Boaz nodded in agreement and smiled, "Indeed, it is a very fine morning."

The other men waited for Boaz to continue, but when he simply sat among them quietly, another spoke up, "We do not typically enjoy your company during the threshing period, Boaz. Have you joined us for a particular reason?"

Boaz looked at the other man and nodded. "Tov comes this way, does he not?"

Some of the men glanced at Boaz with curiosity, but all of them nodded. "He does. He often joins us until the sun reaches its zenith, then he moves on to check on his own land and workers."

Another man asked, "You have business with Tov?"

Boaz replied, "I do."

The first man who had greeted Boaz leaned toward him. "Will you be needing our counsel then?"

Boaz looked at the group of older men, all elders among his people, and noted that there were ten sitting about him. Meeting the first man's clear gaze, Boaz smiled warmly before replying, "I will. I pray that the Lord's will be done this day, and I think your presence will help see that it is."

The other men began to murmur amongst themselves, but none of the men pressed Boaz on the matter. Instead, they drew him into conversation regarding harvest and his fields, and as the conversation flowed, time ebbed onward.

Finally, with the sun high over the eastern horizon, Boaz saw Tov approaching the gate.

"Tov," he said, "come over and sit down."

Tov, Boaz's uncle, smiled widely and moved to join him.

"Boaz! Shalom! We have all been so busy with harvest, it feels as though I haven't seen you in months!"

Boaz reached out and clapped Tov on his shoulder. "It certainly does."

Tov laughed. "I don't see you here. Ever. What brings you to the gate when I know you must have work you would rather be doing?"

Boaz shrugged and looked at the elders gathered about. "Gentlemen? Will you all move closer? Join us?"

As the elders moved and adjusted to sit nearer to Boaz and Tov, Boaz noted the sudden unease on Tov's face. He leaned toward his uncle and whispered, "Fear not. I have something I wish to discuss with you; the elders are just here to make sure I am not mistaken."

Boaz smiled wide and Tov visibly relaxed beside him. Once the elders were settled around them, Boaz started.

"The parcel of land which used to belong to our relative Elimelek is being offered for sale by Naomi, who has returned from the plain of Moab. I thought I should tell you about it. Buy it in the presence of the people sitting here and in the presence of the leaders of my people. If you want to redeem it, redeem it. But if it is not to be redeemed, then tell me so that I can know. Because if there is no one else in line to redeem it, I'm after you."

Tov leaned back and Boaz waited for him to consider his proclamation. Boaz assumed that Tov knew Naomi was back in Ephrathah, and Boaz realized that Tov's own affairs had kept him from learning much about her or Elimelek since she returned. While he waited for Tov to consider the value of Elimelek's lands, Boaz watched his uncle for a sign giving away the way he would decide.

Finally, Tov replied, "I want to redeem it."

Boaz's heart sank, but he nodded. "Very well." He paused a moment and then continued, "I have to also make you aware. The same day you buy the field, you must also marry Ruth, the woman from Moab, the wife of the deceased Mahlon, in order to raise up in the name of the deceased an heir for his property."

Boaz watched the additional news settle on Tov.

"You did know of Ruth, did you not?" one of the elders asked Tov.

Tov shrugged, "I knew what the rumors stated, but nothing more."

Another elder asked, "You've not gone to see Naomi since her return?"

Tov shook his head, "I've simply been too busy."

The elders dropped into silence, and Boaz waited for Tov to consider the added stipulations to purchasing Elimelek's land.

Tov sighed deeply. "Then I can't redeem it for myself because I might put my own inheritance at risk. You take my redemption on yourself because I can't redeem it."

Tov paused a moment, then he reached down and began to untie his sandal. As he did so, he glanced over at Boaz. "You redeem it."

Boaz sat in silence until Tov removed his sandal and handed it to Boaz.

At that point, working hard to keep a smile from his face, Boaz took the sandal from Tov as he addressed everyone who sat around them.

"You are witnesses today that I am purchasing all that belonged to Elimelek, and all that belonged to Kilion and Mahlon. Also, I am acquiring as my wife Ruth, the woman from Moab, the wife of Mahlon, in order to raise up in the name of the deceased an heir for his property so that the name of the deceased will not be cut off from his kinsmen and from the gate of this place." Boaz waved his arm toward all who were around them, "You are witnesses today."

The men gathered about Tov and Boaz nodded in agreement. "We are witnesses. May Adonai make the woman who has come into your house like Rachel and like Leah, who between them built up the house of Israel. Do worthy deeds in Efrat, become renowned in Ephrathah. May your house become like the house of Perez, whom Tamar bore to Judah, because of the seed Adonai will give you from this young woman."

Boaz bowed his head there among the leaders of his people and thanked God for the quick resolution. When he raised his eyes, he met those of Tov, who sat staring at him.

"You know this Ruth, don't you?" Tov asked simply.

"I do. She is a woman I am proud and honored to make my wife."

Tov rose to his feet and shook hands with Boaz. "May God bless you both."

Boaz rose to his feet and pulled Tov in for a strong embrace. "The Lord's will be done."

The men stepped away from each other and nodded at each other with respect.

Boaz watched Tov leave the gates, then he said his thanks and farewell to the elders as an urgency to see Ruth engulfed him.

TWELVE

I wept as the women around me wiped the sweat from my brow and dried my face. Contractions rippled through me, causing me to cry out as the pain nearly overwhelmed me. My mind was focused on the child in my womb. I prayed inwardly over and over that the child be born and born healthy. As I writhed in agony on the blankets while Naomi checked the placement of the baby within me, I fought down the fears and the sadness I felt for every unborn child that had come before when Mahlon had been alive.

As though reading my mind, Naomi rubbed my swollen belly.

"Ruth, my child, God has provided you with another good and loving husband. He has brought us home to Ephrathah where we belong. He has taken you to his bosom and called you His own. He will bless you. He will bless Boaz. He will be with this child."

I opened my eyes to stare at Naomi and saw sudden conviction and promise in my mother-in-law's eyes. As another contraction spasmed through me, I could only nod and grit my teeth even as I gripped the hands of the women next to me.

"Now, Ruth. Push!"

I pushed as hard as I could against the contraction. I pushed so hard I thought I was going to force my insides out, but even as I pushed, I clung to Naomi's words.

Lord, please. Please, be with this child. Lord, please bless its coming into this world. Please let this child honor both Mahlon and Boaz. Please, Lord...

As I continued to push, I vaguely heard Naomi encouraging me, but my mind was struggling between prayers, hope, and dread. I could not bear to lose another child. Yet I hoped. And Naomi believed. My mind and heart swayed back and forth on the waves of pain that wracked my body.

"The baby's head is out, Ruth! Oh! Ruth! Keep pushing, my child! Keep pushing."

I heard Naomi's words break into my muddled thoughts and prayers. I gritted my teeth and bore down, lifting my hips off the blankets, willing the child to emerge.

An instant later, I collapsed in a breathless heap. No tears. No emotions. Just pure exhaustion. As the light of the room registered, and as the murmurs of the women sank in, I thought of the child and I forced myself to lift my head to look at Naomi.

Naomi, still sitting between my legs, had her head bowed low as she worked quickly. I watched my mother-in-law's face for any sign that would indicate if the babe was alive or dead.

After what felt like an eternity to me, Naomi sat up on her knees, a bundle of cloth held tight to her chest. I watched Naomi scoot around on the floor until she was beside me. Carefully, placing the bundle on my chest, Naomi beamed at me. "You have a beautiful son, Ruth. God has given you a beautiful, strong, baby boy!"

Unbelieving, I unwrapped the bundle to see the wide eyes of my newborn son blinking into the light of the room. I unwrapped him a little more and moved him to latch on, and I sighed in relief and thanks. As my son latched on, I fell asleep with a smile on my face.

After a while, I woke as Naomi took the baby from my arms. She nodded to the gathered women and they began to leave the room, one after another. One of the women walking out commented, "Blessed be Adonai, who today has provided you a redeemer!"

Another chimed in, "May his name be renowned in Israel."

A third, "May he restore your life and provide for your old age, for your daughter-in-law, who loves you and is better to you than seven sons, has give birth to him."

As Naomi held the baby close, she looked out of the room. Catching Boaz's eye, she nodded for him to enter.

Boaz came into the room, his eyes flickering over the bundle in Naomi's arms, but then he turned to me and dropped at my side.

"My love..." he started.

I searched his face and saw love and concern in his eyes. He knew of the babies I had lost before, and he worried as much as I did over this whole pregnancy. I reached up and stroked the side of his face.

"I am fine." I looked behind him and nodded at Naomi. "We have a son."

Boaz smiled widely. "We do, and now your first love has an heir. Our Lord has blessed Elimelek's line once more."

I saw Naomi smile wide behind Boaz, her eyes bright with unshed tears. She moved around to my other side and laid the babe in my arms. She looked at Boaz. "This child needs a name."

Boaz nodded and stared at the tiny puckered face. "I cannot..," he murmured. He looked at Naomi. "Ima, what do you think?"

Naomi reached out and took one of the babe's tiny hands in hers. "Obed."

I looked at the little face and rolled the name over in my mind. "What does Obed mean?"

Naomi kept looking at the little bit of perfection in my arms. "I think of this name in honor of you, my daughter. You have been a loving servant to me. Then you became a willing servant to Boaz, first in his fields and now as his wife. Obed means to serve or to become an expert in a skill. My prayer is that this child grows into a man with the same loyal and loving heart of his mother."

Warmth flooded through me at the compliment and the realization that Naomi held me in such high regard. Boaz laid a hand on my arm, and in his eyes, I saw he shared Naomi's feelings.

"Oh, yes! Obed is a fine name," I agreed.

Naomi asked, "Boaz, what do you think? Obed?"

He smiled and nodded. Then he lifted little Obed from my arms and handed the babe to Naomi. "Would you do the honor of announcing your grandson to the world?"

Naomi's eyes twinkled. She took Obed in her arms and stepped out of the room, calling as she went, announcing the birth of Obed, the son of Mahlon, to all who had gathered for the joyous occasion.

EPILOGUE

The Lord said to Samuel, "How long will you mourn for Saul, since I have rejected him as king over Israel? Fill your horn with oil and be on your way; I am sending you to Jesse of Ephrathah. I have chosen one of his sons to be king."

But Samuel said, "How can I go? If Saul hears about it, he will kill me."

The Lord said, "Take a heifer with you and say, 'I have come to sacrifice to the Lord.' Invite Jesse [son of Obed] to the sacrifice, and I will show you what to do. You are to anoint for me the one I indicate."

Samuel did what the Lord said. When he arrived at Ephrathah, the elders of the town trembled when they met him. They asked, "Do you come in peace?"

Samuel replied, "Yes, in peace; I have come to sacri-fice to the Lord. Consecrate yourselves and come

*to the sacrifice with me." Then he consecrated
Jesse and his sons and invited them to the
sacrifice.*

*When they arrived, Samuel saw Eliab and thought,
"Surely the Lord's anointed stands here before the
Lord."*

*But the Lord said to Samuel, "Do not consider his
appearance or his height, for I have rejected him.*

*The Lord does not look at the things people look at.
People look at the outward appearance, but the
Lord looks at the heart."*

*Then Jesse called Abinadab and had him pass in front
of Samuel. But Samuel said, "The Lord has not
chosen this one either."*

*Jesse then had Shammah pass by, but Samuel said,
"Nor has the Lord chosen this one."*

*Jesse had seven of his sons pass before Samuel, but
Samuel said to him, "The Lord has not chosen
these."*

So he asked Jesse, "Are these all the sons you have?"

*"There is still the youngest," Jesse answered. "He is
tending the sheep."*

*Samuel said, "Send for him; we will not sit down
until he arrives."*

*So he sent for him and had him brought in. He was
glowing with health and had a fine appearance
and handsome features.*

*Then the Lord said, "Rise and anoint him; this is the
one."*

So Samuel took the horn of oil and anointed him in

the presence of his brothers, and from that day on the Spirit of the Lord came powerfully upon David.

1 Samuel 16:1-13

GLOSSARY OF TERMS

Abba – Hebrew word for *father*

Boker tov – Hebrew phrase for *good morning*

Chemosh – Moabite god who brought victory in battle

Ehud — Israelite Judge who tricked and killed King Eglon (Book of Judges)

Ephrathah – original name for Bethlehem

Ephrathite- an inhabitant of Ephrathah

Halug – loosely belted tunic

Ima – Hebrew word for *mother*

Isha – Hebrew word for *wife; woman*

King's Highway — ancient trade route from Damascus south to Gulf of Aqaba

Kir-Moab — thought to be the capital of Moab; also known as Kir-hareseth

Shalom – Hebrew word for *hello; goodbye; peace*

Tichel – head covering

Tov – the unnamed brother of Elimelek (some references debate whether Tov was the name or the identifier, as "tov" translates to "good" indicating usage of "tov" may have simply been used as an indication the man was the closest, or best relative to take the role of "redeemer."

Yahweh – vocalization of the four consonants (YHWH) in the way many scholars think this covenant name for God was pronounced in OT times

FAMILY LINE

FAMILY LINE

NAHSHON BEN AMINADAB

ELIMELEK (NAOMI)	SALMON (RAHAB)	NAOMI'S FATHER	TOV-UNNAMED BROTHER
MAHLON (RUTH)	BOAZ (RUTH)	NAOMI	
KILION (ORPAH)	OBED		
	JESSE		
	DAVID		
	(LINE OF CHRIST)		

BIBLIOGRAPHY

Abarim Publications. "The Amazing Name Obed: Meaning and Etymology." *Abarim Publications*, Abarim Publications, https://www.abarim-publications.com/Meaning/Obed.html.

The Book of Ruth Summary - Chabad.org. https://www.chabad.org/library/article_cdo/aid/2890/jewish/The-Book-of-Ruth-Summary.htm.

"Encyclopedia Britannica." *Encyclopedia Britannica*, britannica.com.

Encyclopedia of the Bible - Bible Gateway, https://www.biblegateway.com/resources/encyclopedia-of-the-bible/.

Halley, Henry H. *Halley's Bible Handbook / Classic Edition*. Zondervan, 2014.

Karssen, Gien. "Naomi." *Her Name Is Woman: Book 2*, Navpress, Colorado Springs, CO, 1977.

Karssen, Gien. "Ruth." *Her Name Is Woman: Book 2*, Navpress, Colorado Springs, CO, 1977.

Keener, Craig S., and John H. Walton. "Ruth." *NKJV, Cultural Backgrounds Study Bible*, Zondervan, Grand Rapids, MI, 2017.

Matthews, Victor Harold. *The Cultural World of the Bible: An Illustrated Guide to Manners and Customs*. Baker Academic, 2015.

My Jewish Learning. "Hebrew Words." *My Jewish Learning*, 15 Sept. 2022, https://www.myjewishlearning.com/article/hebrew-words/.

Nelson's Three-in-One Bible Reference Companion. T. Nelson, 1993.

Packer, J. I., and Merrill C. Tenney. *Illustrated Manners and Customs of the Bible*. T. Nelson, 1997.

Peterson, Eugene. "Ruth." *Message Bible: Leatherlike Brown, Personal Size*, Tyndale House Publishers, 2014.

Phillips, Don T. *The Book of Ruth: Historical and Prophetic Truths*. Virtual Bookworm Publishing Co., 2016.

Rose Book of Bible Charts. Rose Publishing, 2017.

"Ruth Rabbah." *Sefaria*, https://www.sefaria.org/Ruth_Rabbah.

Sobel, Rabbi Jason. "Hebrew Word Study with Rabbi Jason Sobel." *Fusion Global with Rabbi Jason Sobel*, 6 May 2022, https://www.fusionglobal.org/connections/hebrew-word-study/.

Stern, David H., and Barry A. Rubin. "Ruth." *The Complete Jewish Study Bible: Insights for Jews & Christians: Illuminating the Jewishness of God's Word*, Hendrickson Bibles, Peabody, MA, 2016.

Watts, J. Wash. *Old Testament Teaching*. Broadman Press, 1967.

Wright, Paul H. *Rose Then and Now Bible Atlas*. Rose Publishing, 2013.

ABOUT THE AUTHOR

A voracious bookworm since childhood, C. Borden has a deep love for reading and writing. Raised in a Bible-believing home and educated within multiple denominational schools and colleges, she continually searches to learn more about the history and culture of her faith.

When she is not writing or curled up with a good book, C. Borden is active with her family, working in her garden, or exploring the mountains around her Montana home.

Connect with C. Borden

Official Website:
www.authorcborden.com
Monthly Newsletter:
https://dl.bookfunnel.com/130ifx4mpk

Printed in Great Britain
by Amazon